RELUC

Since she had been widowed six years
ago, Eleanor had been very cautious
about her relationships with men; they
were only too ready to assume that all
widows were merry ones! And James
Ramsay was precisely the kind of man
most likely to jump to this conclusion.
So Eleanor decided it might be best to
leave him with his wrong impressions
about her . . .

# RELUCTANT PARAGON

BY

## CATHERINE GEORGE

**MILLS & BOON LIMITED**
15–16 BROOK'S MEWS
LONDON W1A 1DR

*First published 1982*
*Australian copyright 1982*
*Philippine copyright 1982*
*This edition 1982*

© Catherine George 1982

ISBN 0 263 74083 8

*Set in Monophoto Plantin 10 on 11½ pt.*
*01-1182 – 51404*

*Made and printed in Great Britain by*
*Richard Clay (The Chaucer Press) Ltd,*
*Bungay, Suffolk*

# CHAPTER ONE

ELEANOR was oblivious to the blue and gold beauty of the crisp October morning as she carefully coaxed her elderly, reluctant little car into one of the few parking spaces remaining in the market square. The chimes from St Margaret's Church struck the quarter after nine, and she groaned as she locked the car and set off at a punishing pace up the busy square and turned into Westgate Street. She fairly sprinted the last hundred yards past the Law Courts and up the steps of one of the tall Georgian houses opposite, where the early morning sun glinted on the gold lettering of the name 'Ramsay & Coulter, Consulting Engineers' on the graceful fanlight over the door.

The elegant hall that had once been the setting for rout parties and soirées was now full of Monday morning bustle, telephones ringing at the switchboard and the Telex clattering as she hurried towards the stairs, almost colliding en route with Frances Marshall, Mr Coulter's secretary, who put out a steadying hand.

'You're late, Eleanor—car trouble again?'

'Need you ask!' said Eleanor, out of breath. 'Is Mr Ramsay in yet?'

'He was here before half-past eight this morning, apparently.'

'Lord! Thanks, Fran, see you later.'

Eleanor flew up the stairs as fast as the high heels of her elegant suede boots allowed, and dived into the small staff cloakroom. Ignoring her customary coat-hanger, she flung her jacket on to a peg and inspected her flushed cheeks in the mirror with disapproval, smoothing the shining coil of bright brown hair. The olive-tinted face frowning back at her had a pointed chin and high cheekbones beneath wide dark eyes that were sparkling from the enforced exercise. She checked a short straight nose for shine, added a touch of lip-gloss to the full curves of a generous mouth, then made herself stand perfectly still for a count of ten. Poise restored, Eleanor went along the landing to the door marked 'Senior Partner.' Hector Ramsay was standing at the tall window as she went in, looking down at the busy street, a frown on his face. He was a large man, well over six feet tall, with a burly physique and a great shock of white hair, who wore his sixty-odd years with panache.

'Good morning, Eleanor,' he said, a twinkle in his bright blue eyes, 'come and sit down. No, don't get your notebook, I want to talk to you.'

'Good morning, Mr Ramsay, I'm sorry I'm late . . .'

'You don't have to tell me, girl,' he interrupted, 'I just enjoyed watching you legging it down the street. I suppose that damned contraption of yours wouldn't start again this morning. You know, Eleanor, if that car were a dog you'd have had it put down long ago.'

She laughed ruefully.

'I know, I know! If it hadn't been for Ted, who lives next door to my landlady, I wouldn't be here yet. He did something mysterious under the bonnet, told me to get in while the engine was running and drive without stopping until I reached town. Luckily the lights were green as I came up Castle Hill. I gave him the spare keys and he's going to collect it later on and take it in to the garage where he works to see if they'll give me something for it. I expect it will be just the scrap value, but whatever it is will be reserved solely for bus fares. No way am I continuing to start every day seething with frustration.'

Her employer eyed her knowingly.

'Don't care for parting with that poise of yours, do you, girl?'

'You're so right, Mr Ramsay—and I do apologise for being late so often recently. It won't happen again from now on.'

Hector Ramsay sat down heavily behind his desk and looked at her for a few moments, then he sighed.

'No use putting it off any longer, Eleanor. There's something I have to get off my chest, so I may as well get on with it.'

Eleanor's head lifted sharply, her eyes troubled.

'No, nothing to do with you, my dear—a man couldn't ask for a better secretary, and well you know it. No, the trouble is all on my side. To put it in a nutshell I'm forced to go out to grass; doctor's orders. I've been battling with blood pressure for a while, only they call it hypertension these days, or some such. Now the old ticker's going haywire as well, so I'm giving up the reins and taking to gardening and walking the dog with Margaret.'

Eleanor sat stunned.

'Mr Ramsay, I'm at a complete loss,' she said finally. 'Forgive me for all that stupid chat about the car, when all the time you were waiting to tell me this. I had no idea there was anything wrong. You've always been the most energetic person I know—of any age.' Something suddenly occurred to her. 'May I know who will take your place?'

'As you know, son James runs the London office and deals with all the overseas business. For the present he'll divide his time between the Midlands and London until things are sorted out. There's no problem these days in getting from A to B. He gets here in a couple of hours up the M1 in that new high-powered car of his; showy thing, but it can certainly move. Anyway, he'll be here for a couple of weeks to start with.'

Eleanor was assailed by a chill feeling of insecurity.

'This is terribly sudden, Mr Ramsay,' she said quietly, 'it's difficult to take in. Does this mean you won't be coming to the office at all after today? Won't you work with your son for a time until he settles in?'

'Lord, no!' Hector Ramsay laughed. 'James is the last person to need his hand held. I think the world of him, and I respect him as a damned fine man at his job, but he won't run in harness, and I don't blame him. He can talk things over with me in the evenings for a bit, if necessary; he's living at home with us for a few days. Margaret says the redecorations he wanted aren't quite finished at his own cottage.'

Eleanor was silent, a sudden lump in her throat. The man opposite looked across the desk fondly.

'Margaret said I should have let you know from the beginning,' he said apologetically, 'but I didn't want you watching me like a hawk and imagining imminent cardiac arrest every time I coughed. No, lass, it's better this way, and I'm not exactly emigrating. I'll be in from time to time.'

Eleanor stood up, straightening her back and squaring her shoulders, a characteristic mannerism that Hector Ramsay noted with affection.

'Will Mr—will your son wish to keep me on as his secretary?' Eleanor asked a little stiffly.

Her employer rose to his feet and wagged an admonishing finger in her troubled face.

'Did you have any doubts on the score? I hope not, my girl. He wouldn't find as good a secretary as you in a hurry. Besides, he's going to need someone who knows the ropes, and I've trained you well.'

'Nevertheless, Mr Ramsay, it's more than possible that your son will want a secretary of his own choice. He may not like me. Perhaps I don't meet his particular requirements.'

He stared at her in blank astonishment.

'Eleanor,' he said patiently, 'James is an intelligent man, a damned good engineer, and, as far as I know, a pretty good judge of character. Of course he'll consider you suitable. He'd be a halfwit if he didn't, and while James may be many other things, a halfwit he is not, as you'll no doubt discover for youself before very long.'

Hector's last words were obviously meant to be re-assuring, but they gave Eleanor a distinct feeling of apprehension.

'Very well, Mr Ramsay, I'll do everything I possibly can, of course. But I shall miss you very much.' She looked up at him, her big brown eyes candid. 'These three years with you have been a marvellous and in-valuable experience, and I very much regret things can't continue the way they are.'

'No more than I do, lass.' His voice was gruff. 'We've hit it off tolerably well together, you and I. You were such a remote, quiet young thing when you came, all those frightening qualifications and no ex-perience at all. But I knew you would be right for the job. I told Margaret as much the day you started. Anyway, lass, this won't do.' He took a gold hunter from his pocket. 'The time's going on. Got to see the doctor at ten-thirty, so I must be on my way. James will be here at two. You can sort out the mail, and if you run out of work there's the revised McGlusky report to get on with.'

He came round the desk and took her hand, squeezed it hard, then he was gone.

Eleanor went slowly through the connecting door into her own small office like someone in a trance. She sat down at her desk and stared unseeingly at the pile of paperwork in front of her, then gave a long and heartfelt sigh. This was turning out to be a Monday of Mondays, and it had barely begun. She opened and sorted letters mechanically, the prospect of Hector Ramsay's son as her boss overshadowing her thoughts. She knew that he visited his family some weekends, which were generally working sessions with his father, and seldom visited the office in Westgate Street. The last time had been when Eleanor was on her annual leave. James Ramsay would have to be something quite out of the ordinary to fill Hector Ramsay's shoes, she reflected.

She went on with her normal tasks with the precision of long practice, and disposed of everything she could do independently. She then went into Mr Ramsay's office and made sure that the beautifully proportioned room was in perfect order. She tidied the desk, leaving one basket of letters for James Ramsay's signature, another to be opened by him personally, and a third containing the routine mail for him to look over. Back at her desk there was the waiting report to get on with, and she began to type furiously, glad to immerse herself in routine.

She was more than glad to welcome Frances, who appeared promptly at eleven with two cups of coffee, a look of intense excitement on her face.

'Had you any idea about poor Mr Ramsay, Eleanor?' she asked. 'Mr Coulter just told me. He also said that the heir apparent is taking over pro tem. When will he be starting?'

'In about three hours' time,' said Eleanor despondently, drinking her coffee. 'Do you know him, Fran? I've always missed him on his rare appearances here.'

'Well, love, for a start you're going to be the envy of the neighbourhood, or at least the female population.'

'How nice,' said Eleanor with resignation. 'That sort, is he?'

'Well, of course, you wouldn't know if you've never met him. When James was younger he was the darling of all the young things in town, and most of them in a twenty-mile radius outside it. Then he got engaged and they all had to retire from the lists.'

'Really? What does he do with his wife on his travels; drag her with him?'

'Oh, he never actually married. It was quite a nine-day wonder at the time. He'd bought a beautiful cottage, one of those down in Castle Reach, with a garden backing on to the river and looking up on the Castle. He furnished it just as she wanted it, everything was set for the wedding, then she threw him over for some elderly tycoon with a great deal more money. They say James has been a bit cynical about the ladies since; hardly to be wondered at, really.'

'He sounds a fascinating prospect as an employer, Frances, sort of a combination whizz-kid and misogynist. There's a nasty cold feeling in the pit of my stomach.'

'He's not a kid, though, Eleanor, he must be in his early thirties, I suppose. You know, you do look a bit worn this morning.'

'Nervous tension,' said Eleanor, tersely. 'Come on, Frances, clear out, I have a lot to do.'

'All right, love,' said Frances sympathetically, 'come and have lunch at Mario's.'

'No, thanks, but perhaps you'd bring me back a

sandwich. I'll work through, I think. Everything is going to be super-perfect for the new boss.' She yawned widely. 'Lord, I must get to bed early tonight. These weekends at my sister's are getting too much. Her social life flattens me!'

Frances laughed.

'You know you'd hate it if you didn't go off there most weekends.'

'You're right, but I can't help feeling wistful about a whole weekend to myself, just pottering. Complete bliss! I adore my niece and nephews, but Frances, they're so relentlessly energetic. Even the baby has me fielding an endless stream of missiles from the pram. Anyway, lovely as this is, Frances, shoo! I really must get on.'

Her friend retreated, laughing, then popped her head back round the door.

'I forgot to mention that James is quite a dish in an austere, dark sort of way.'

'That's supposed to comfort me, I imagine?'

Frances departed, grinning.

After Eleanor had eaten her lunchtime sandwich, she had another quick look around the Senior Partner's office, straightening a chair, fiddling with the baskets of correspondence until she had fidgeted herself into a state of tension. Finally she retreated to the cloakroom and took down her long mane of hair, brushing it vigorously. This calmed her somewhat, and she restored the shining length to its usual impeccable coil. After a long impartial look in the mirror she decided her slim rust-coloured tweed skirt and cream silk shirt printed in the same shade of rust looked both elegant and efficient. She was more doubtful about her knee-length brown suède boots, which were possibly a thought frivolous. Not that there was much to be done about that, short of meeting the new boss in her stockinged feet. She grinned at the thought, then decided it was no use prolonging the agony, squared her shoulders and went out to confront the enemy. She was half relieved, half disappointed when it was Hector Ramsay's voice that bade her enter in answer to her knock on his door.

'Hello, Eleanor, forgot a few personal belongings.' He smiled up at her sheepishly from behind the desk. 'Thought I'd better leave the drawers empty of my rubbish ready for James. He'll be along in a minute, I left him talking to John Coulter.'

'I thought you were he.' Eleanor felt a decided sense of anti-climax. 'I've put everything ready for him.'

'I can see that, lass.' Hector came round the desk and handed her a small package, putting an arm round her shoulders. 'I really came back to give you this, Eleanor, as a small appreciation for all those hours of overtime you put in for me. Margaret had it made for you at that place in the High Street, and I collected it lunchtime.'

Eleanor looked dumbly at the contents of the small jeweller's box in her hand. Coiled round a raised bed of velvet was a gold chain, with a pendant hanging from it, a small gold initial E studded with garnets.

'Mrs Ramsay even remembered my birthstone.' Eleanor's voice was unsteady. Suddenly her control deserted her and she turned her face into his shoulder, unable to hold back a few uncharacteristic tears.

'Now then, buck up, lass,' said Mr Ramsay in surprise. 'Where's that well-known self-control gone? Here, mop yourself with this handkerchief.'

She obeyed, smiling damply, and tried to thank him, when a deep, cold voice spoke from the doorway, making her spring apart from her employer.

'Forgive me if I intrude, Father, but if you're not too occupied perhaps you could make the necessary introduction.'

Eleanor felt as though cubes of ice were cascading down her spine as she looked at the man in the doorway. James Ramsay was as tall as his father, but much slimmer, with an air of polished, whipcord elegance. She gained a quick impression of a superbly tailored grey suit, dark hair expertly cut to just above his collar, and a tanned face with an arrogant, aquiline nose. The expression of hostility and distaste in the heavy-lidded eyes burned indelibly in Eleanor's mind for hours afterwards.

She became aware of Mr Ramsay talking to his son, his voice full of suppressed amusement.

'That'll do, James, you know very well that this must be Eleanor; Eleanor Hunt, the best secretary I've ever had. Now she's all yours, mind you take care of her.' His eyes twinkled as he turned to her. 'I'm sure you and James will get on well, my dear—be sure to show him the ropes, even though he'll be inclined to think he knows them all better than you! See you tonight, James. Goodbye, my dear.'

He clapped his son on the shoulder and closed the door loudly, leaving behind him an atmosphere that was a great deal short of cordial.

James Ramsay strolled across the room slowly, studying Eleanor as he approached. Like someone in the throes of a nightmare she stood, her feet welded to the carpet and every instinct screaming for flight. Her fingers clenched around the small jeweller's box, which had suddenly assumed packing-case proportions. His eyes dropped to it as he held out his hand with cold courtesy. Eleanor came to life as she hastily transferred her unexpected, and momentarily unwelcome, gift to her left hand so that she could take the one he offered with her right. Dropping it after the briefest perfunctory moment, he said in that deep, rather harsh voice with its glacial undertone:

'As you've already gathered, I'm James Ramsay. How do you do, Miss Hunt. Please sit down, and perhaps we can begin to put each other in the picture.'

Eleanor moved to the chair in front of the desk while he went behind it to seat himself in his father's chair. Usurper! thought Eleanor with resentment, but sat composedly while those cold eyes surveyed her intently.

'So you are my father's paragon, Miss Hunt,' he began conversationally. 'He really is a wily old fox. When he mentioned you he managed, in some abstract, subtle way, to convey an impression of extreme efficiency, coupled with advancing years, hornrimmed spectacles and shapeless tweed.'

Eleanor stiffened. The word 'paragon' became definitely derogatory issuing from that well-cut mouth, and she felt her cheeks flushing.

Still looking at her with the same considering expression, he went on:

'You look about twenty-one. I see no spectacles, and while that very elegant skirt is, I believe, possibly tweed, not your worst enemy could call it shapeless. This, of course, I can see with my own eyes. The efficiency, Miss Hunt, can only be proved by you yourself in due course.'

Rigidly controlling the feeling of outrage threatening to consume her, Eleanor looked coolly across the desk at him.

'Mr Ramsay, I'm aware that your father has handed me over to you willy-nilly. If you dislike the arrangement, and wish to engage a secretary of your own choice . . .'

'You don't want to work for me?' he cut in sharply.

'I didn't say that. I was trying to make it clear that if you wanted to replace me, I would naturally stay on until you find someone suitable, if that were a more acceptable arrangement to you.'

'My dear Miss Hunt,' he drawled, tilting himself back in his chair, 'my father is in no way to be upset at this particular juncture, and if I went home tonight with the news that I was ridding myself of his paragon I've no doubt that would precipitate the very crisis we're all at some pains to avoid. Not to mention the fact that my mother would have my head!'

The word 'paragon' was beginning to make Eleanor itch between her shoulder blades, but she asked quietly.

'You want me to carry on as usual, then?'

'I do indeed. Perhaps you would be good enough to fill me in on your qualifications, etc. Father was somewhat vague, though I gather this is your first job.'

'Yes. I came here straight from college almost three years ago. I gained a First in English at the university here and decided to combine a commercial course with it rather than research, or teach, and I've never had any leaning towards journalism. I took Portuguese as my extra subject, and I type sixty words per minute, also I can take shorthand verbatim, though I'm more comfortable at a slightly slower speed. My references came from my university Professor and the local doctor from the village where I used to live in Cheshire.'

He shot a sardonic glance at her, then murmured,

'Very, very impressive; one could hardly ask for more. Did my father dictate directly to you, or use a tape recorder?'

'Directly to me, as he liked to wander round the

room, though if you prefer to use a machine I'm perfectly accustomed to audio work.'

'My dear Miss Hunt, I never doubted it for a moment!'

The gleam was more pronounced, but Eleanor by this time had herself well in hand, in complete possession of her customary calm, and felt quite impervious to any shafts of sarcasm he might feel inclined to let fly.

'Now to business,' he said briskly. 'Perhaps you will elucidate on this enormous amount of paper on the desk, and tell how you normally deal with it.'

'The volume is always much greater on a Monday, of course,' Eleanor began. 'This pile consists of all mail marked personal, or of a confidential nature. These I leave for you to open. The rest is divided into those letters I'm able to deal with myself, which I bring to you for your perusal and signature. The rest are the routine things which I send to the typing pool, and which are returned for my signature. Also I type your reports, but if the work-load becomes a bit heavy, or there's a deadline to meet, I sometimes pass on some of the less confidential ones to the pool after I've typed them myself to rough-draft stage. This would be done only with your sanction, of course.'

'Of course,' he agreed, 'though you make it sound as if I'm slightly on the superfluous side.'

Eleanor smiled politely, and waited while he looked through her share of the mail.

'Fair enough, Miss Hunt, you take off your share of the spoils and deal with them in the usual way, while I sort through the rest. When can I expect tea?'

'I usually bring in a tea-tray at three-thirty.'

'Good. When you do, bring yourself a cup and your notebook and I'll dictate.'

Eleanor inclined her head and rose to pick up the basket of mail. The jewellery box fell to the floor with a small thump, and she retrieved it hastily, hoping it had escaped his notice.

It had not.

'A token of my father's esteem, Miss Hunt?' he asked, his voice expressionless.

'A parting gift.' Eleanor was equally colourless. She went unhurriedly across the room to her office, but before reaching the door she paused for a moment, then turned to face James Ramsay, whose eyes were still fixed on her unwaveringly.

'Two very minor details, Mr Ramsay,' said Eleanor coolly, 'I'm twenty-four, not twenty-one, and actually it's *Mrs* Hunt.'

The man behind the desk stared for a time at the door that had closed very gently behind the small, straight-backed figure of his newly-acquired secretary, then he shrugged irritably and applied himself to the daunting pile of paperwork in front of him.

# CHAPTER TWO

By seven-thirty that evening no one was left in the building as Eleanor came wearily down the graceful sweep of the staircase. The elegant hall below served as both reception area and showcase for the company. The panelled walls held mahogany-framed glass cases containing lavish colour representations of former successful projects. Comfortable leather settees either side of the main entrance allowed waiting clients a view of three scale models—an airline terminal, a luxury hotel, complete with swimming pool and tropical gardens perfect down to the last palm tree, and at the back of the hall, under the curve of the staircase, in pride of place was a section of an oil refinery with its intricate convolutions of minuscule pipes all in accurate detail.

Tonight Eleanor passed them all blindly. She closed and locked the big door behind her and set out for the bus stop, to wait in apathy until the bus came along. She arrived eventually at the top of Mill Crescent and walked down it swiftly, shivering in the chill evening breeze. As she let herself in to No. 18 her landlady emerged from her sitting-room, her kind face full of concern.

'You've had a long day, Eleanor—bad one, was it, dear?'

'Mrs Jenkins, that's an understatement—I'm on my knees! I'll tell you all about it tomorrow, but right now all I can think about is collapsing on my settee.'

'I hope you're going to eat something first! Anyway,

you have a visitor—no, no, don't look so horrified, it's only your sister. I let her into your flat about ten minutes ago. She's put her car into the garage not to waste the lights.'

'You had me worried there for a moment!' Eleanor let out a sigh. 'Oh, by the way, I don't suppose young Ted left any message about the car?'

'Of course! I quite forgot all about it. The garage will go to sixty pounds he said.' Mrs Jenkins's face beamed. 'I thought you'd be pleased.'

'Pleased? Mrs J., that's the best news I've had all day! If I don't see Ted tomorrow give him this fiver and tell him I'll remember him in my prayers. See you, Mrs J.'

The door to her upstairs flat was open, an appetising smell wafting out from the kitchen. Strains of Ravel were coming from the record-player and the low table in front of the couch held cutlery, sliced French bread and a bottle of wine.

'Harriet,' called Eleanor, wearily stripping off her raincoat, 'I'm home!'

Her sister emerged from the kitchen, smiling gleefully at Eleanor's look of enquiry.

'Thought I'd surprise you, darling. We never managed a moment together the whole weekend, and when I rang earlier and found you weren't even home yet I thought I'd do my Lady Bountiful bit. So I packed my basket with goodies and here I am.'

Eleanor subsided limply on to the settee and watched her sister quickly dart to and from the kitchen.

At thirty-four, Harriet was an infinite pleasure to look at. Hair the colour of ripe chestnuts rioted wildly over her shoulders. Big brown eyes were brimful of zest and love for everything, her husband, her children and sister, and life in general. Her figure was the wiry, slender type that looked good in anything, which at the moment was black velvet dungarees worn over a yellow muslin shirt, and topped by a large black shiny plastic apron bearing the scarlet legend 'Kissing don't last, cooking do.'

'Harriet, who is seeing to the children—and even if someone is, it still escapes me as to why you're here tonight when it's only a day since I saw you last. Besides, I never see you in the week anyway, barring emergency.'

'But Eleanor, this *is* an emergency. I came in to town this afternoon for food and who should I meet but Mrs Ramsay. So we had tea together in that little home-made place, and wasn't it expensive, and she told me all about the upheaval. I mean Hector's heart, poor man, and having to retire and his son James taking over, and she was very worried about your being upset, and hoped you'd take to working for James and . . .'

'For pity's sake take a breath, Harriet!' begged Eleanor. 'You still haven't said who's coping with your lot.'

'Richard,' said Harriet. 'I've dealt with Victoria and put her to bed, and I've fed Edward, Charles and David who are now, I trust, watching that science fiction thing on the television. Richard will only have to see them off to bed, and possibly load the dishwasher. Obviously he's not on call tonight.'

'I bet he wishes he were,' said Eleanor drily. 'From the gorgeous smell I gather you brought some soup in your basket.'

'Home-made chicken and leek. I brought this too.' Harriet poured some of the wine into a glass and put it in Eleanor's hand. 'Drink that and I'll bring in the supper. I brought some prawn quiche to follow the soup—a bit of spoiling won't come amiss this evening, by the look of you. In return you can tell me all.'

Eleanor drank some wine, then sat upright to peer at the label on the bottle as Harriet set a bowl of steaming chicken soup in front of her.

'That was some basket! Do you mean you've actually brought some of Richard's best Burgundy for us to hog all on our own? Does he know?'

'Of course not. He'll just think he miscalculated next time we have to entertain one of the consultants. Heavens, Eleanor, what's that round your neck? It's beautiful!'

'You may well ask. It was Mr Ramsay's parting gift, in appreciation of—oh, I don't know, the way we've always worked well together, I suppose. I was so overcome I actually wept on his shoulder.'

'You cried, Eleanor?' Harriet's eyes were searching as her soup-spoon remained suspended half way to its destination. 'That's a shade unusual.'

'It became increasingly more unusual. James Ramsay interrupted us in mid-embrace, as it were, for his first introduction to his new secretary, who disengaged herself hurriedly, looking the picture of guilt and wishing she could crawl under the carpet.'

'That *was* a little unfortunate. Here, have some quiche.'

'It was disastrous. And old Hector enjoyed it enormously, making not the slightest attempt to explain. The new boss and I eventually simmered down into something like a truce. He was very polite, of course, Miss Hunt this and Miss Hunt that, and he kept on referring to his father's "paragon" with a slight air of distaste.'

'Did you enlighten him eventually? Why didn't he notice your wedding ring?'

'It was on the hand that was trying to hide the

jewellery box in a fold of my skirt while we had our little introductory skirmish. He now appears to have the impression that I'm a gold-digger on the make for his father, and when I explained that he should refer to me as "Mrs" Hunt there was an extremely odd expression on his face indeed. I have the distinct feeling he's added a complaisant husband to my score; one who's quite happy about the whole set-up.'

Harriet was entranced.

'How priceless! Eleanor the designing hussy! Richard will fall about.'

'It seems quite funny now, but at the time my sense of humour vanished completely,' sighed Eleanor. 'I can't remember being so angry for years. There was a moment when I had to resist an overwhelming urge to assault him with the rock crystal paperweight on his desk. The man began applying the whip immediately he arrived; he should be called Simon Legree, not James Ramsay. Don't count on my coming over next weekend, Harriet, it's more than likely I shall be working on Saturday.'

Harriet gathered up dishes thoughtfully.

'Just collapse there, love, I'll do these. Do you mind instant coffee? I don't think I'd better wait for the percolator. Incidentally, you haven't said what he's actually like?'

'I'd rather have tea, thanks.' Eleanor stretched out on the settee thankfully. 'He's tall, dark and sort of superior-looking, with those sort of eyes that seem half-closed all the time. Aquiline nose like a Roman emperor, clever, confident, acid and ruthless too, I wouldn't mind betting.'

Harriet brought the tea-tray in and put it down in front of Eleanor.

'Well, love, he certainly seems to have made quite

an impression. Do you like him?'

Eleanor poured the tea carefully.

'I don't think "like" is a word one would apply to James Ramsay,' she said slowly. 'He antagonises me and makes me apprehensive. You know, Harriet, I think things are going to be very different in the company from now on. He's like a tidal wave rushing in over a beach and rearranging the whole shoreline. Oh, heavens, take no notice of me, I'm tired and fanciful. Drink your tea, and then you must return to the bosom of your family. I'm having an early night to try and psych myself up for tomorrow.'

They chatted desultorily about the children for a few minutes, then Harriet jumped up.

'Well, I'm off, love. I'll go and get my basket. Make the rest of the wine into ice-cubes and use them at your leisure for your next foray into French cuisine. Don't mention that to Richard, though, or he'll go off me.'

'And pigs might fly,' said Eleanor fondly. 'Go home before he's on the phone demanding your return. You know how twitched he gets when you drive after dark. Tell him I very much appreciated the company of his wife for an hour, I've completely unwound, you might almost say unravelled, and I think I shall sleep tonight after all.'

'Darling, he doesn't keep me in a cage!' Harriet was indignant. 'Anyway, I wouldn't have been satisfied with a phone call, and you'd probably have gone off to bed without anything to eat. In any case it was practically cheaper to do it this way, discounting the Burgundy, of course.'

Eleanor laughed and held the basket out as Harriet slung a scarlet wool cape round her shoulders.

'Good grief, Harriet, with that basket and the cape

you're Red Riding Hood, not Lady Bountiful!'

'Rather sweet, isn't it? Goodnight, and good luck for tomorrow. Mind you, Eleanor, I must make one observation. You look utterly shattered, I agree, but at least you look alive. You've lost what Richard calls your "*princesse lointaine*" look.'

'My what?'

'I thought it was a bit erudite too, but you know what he means. Anyway, darling, I'm going—give me a ring later in the week, and for heaven's sake don't forget to eat.'

Darling Harriet, thought Eleanor later, as she stood under the shower. When their parents died, first her mother, then years later her father, Harriet had shouldered the responsibility of guardian with great success, never smothering, always ready to provide whatever Eleanor needed, sympathy, hospitality, or sometimes just to be left to herself. Nevertheless it was not Harriet's expressive face that surfaced in her mind just before she slept. The face was dark, masculine and hostile.

Next morning Eleanor was up earlier than usual, determined to eat a proper breakfast and leave herself plenty of time for the unaccustomed bus journey. She made a special effort to be even more well-groomed than usual, mentally exhorting herself to keep her wits honed to a sharp edge. She looked at herself with a little smile when she was dressed. Grey flannel skirt and waistcoat over a black-and-white striped shirt with a white collar, pale grey tights and black Gucci-type shoes were not precisely mourning, but were very definitely not festive either. Finally, after a moment's hesitation, Eleanor defiantly fastened on the new pendant hoping it would act as a talisman.

When she arrived in Ramsay & Coulter's reception

hall that morning she was able to appreciate its charm in her usual way, and stopped to have a word with Louise at the reception desk with its small switchboard. Louise smiled.

'You're early today, Eleanor. Your mail's gone up already.'

'Who took it up, Louise? It's barely eight-thirty.'

'Mr Ramsay. Mr *James* Ramsay.' Louise giggled, smoothing back her hair. 'He came in like a whirlwind, wanting to know my name, what time everyone started, had anything come in on the Telex, all sorts of things.'

'Time I was on my way, then.'

Eleanor's voice was brisker than the way she felt. Firmly controlling the urge to run up the stairs, she mounted them at a moderate pace, took a minute or two in the cloakroom to check on her appearance, then made her way along the landing to her small office. A glance at her watch confirmed that she was a good ten minutes early, but she was determined to be at her desk before her presence was sought.

She looked at her desk with resignation. The usual concentration of envelopes of all sizes lay before her, and she set about them with rapidity, quickly sorting the contents into their requisite baskets. After five minutes the buzzer sounded on her phone and she picked it up gingerly as though it were explosive.

'Mrs Hunt,' she said crisply. 'Good morning.'

'Good morning. Will you come in, please.' The deep voice was a shade peremptory, she thought, but otherwise not too hostile. Eleanor collected her notebook and the basket of confidential mail and went through the communicating door into the other office.

James Ramsay stood in much the same place as his father had the morning before, and Eleanor felt a momentary twinge of resentment as the slimmer, tauter figure turned at her quiet approach. He looked appraisingly at her.

'You keep early hours, Mrs Hunt. The girl at the reception desk said that the female office staff usually start at nine.'

'Yes, sir, that's perfectly true, but normally I prefer to arrive a little earlier and do my sorting out before the phone starts ringing.'

'Highly commendable. Let's not waste your advantage, then, Mrs Hunt. First I would like you to inform my partner, the associate partners, the three senior men in the Drawing Office, also the Company Secretary, that they're to attend a meeting here in my office at eleven. You might ask them to have their coffee before they arrive. You will please sit in on the meeting and record it—not particularly in minute form, more as a report. I don't expect it to run on into the lunch-hour. If it does you may return to work later this afternoon.'

'Yes, sir. Do you wish me to telephone or distribute memos?'

'Telephone, please, and stress that I would be obliged if everyone concerned would make themselves available, regardless of prior commitments.'

'Very well, sir. Shall I do this immediately and return in, say, half an hour for your dictation?'

'Thank you, no. I intend to have a word with John Coulter before the meeting. When I need you I'll buzz. I'm sure you have more than enough to get on with.'

'I do indeed, sir.'

'Mrs Hunt,' he said very softly, looking at her with menace. Eleanor's back straightened defensively as she looked at him coolly. 'For God's sake stop calling me "sir!" ' he grated.

'Of course, Mr Ramsay.' Her face was impassive as

she returned to her office, but when she was alone she indulged in the luxury of a gleeful little smile all to herself.

At eleven sharp all the men summoned to James Ramsay's preliminary meeting grouped themselves round the highly-polished antique desk, and listened intently to the incisive voice that spoke with such lucid authority.

Eleanor, on a small chair to the left of the desk, paid rapt attention as her pencil flew over the pages of her notebook, keeping pace with the words that were spelling out a whole new way of life for Ramsay & Coulter. With articulate clarity the new head of the firm outlined the position of the Midlands office, which, in the present time of recession was overmanned and under-employed. The London office, on the other hand, which dealt mainly with overseas commitments, was expanding, and in need of new staff.

'I need hardly go further, gentlemen, without your realising what I have in mind. At least one-third of the work-force of the operation here is needed in London. Whether they all wish to move remains to be seen. It will be necessary, of course, to decide on which men should be transferred, mainly in the Drawing Office, and some in both the electrical and mechanical areas. Most of the posts to be filled are at junior level, and I imagine can be offered to those of the staff who are still single, or, if married, have no family, or at least children of pre-school age. This will simplify relocation problems. I will give a list of posts to each of you, and I shall expect a list of probable candidates from you in return—if possible, before five this evening.

'Tomorrow, and for the rest of the week, I shall conduct the necessary interviews. By the end of two weeks I hope to have the modified staff deployment for this base well in hand, also the London new look completed.'

Eleanor listened with shock as her pencil automatically flew to keep time with the deep, clipped voice. It soon became clear that for the time being James Ramsay would run both the London and the Midland operation, but that early in the New Year he would be returning permanently to London, and the extensive foreign travel the operation there entailed. John Coulter would then head up the Midlands Office.

Eventually the meeting broke up, just before one o'clock. Eleanor gathered up her notebook and pencils and prepared to leave.

'Just one moment, Mrs Hunt,' said James Ramsay as the door closed behind the others. 'I imagine this has all come as something of a shock to you.'

'I would be less than honest if I said no.' Eleanor paused at the door. 'Naturally I didn't expect you to remain in charge up here indefinitely, but I can only applaud the idea of transferring work-force to London.'

'Come back and sit down for a moment.' He pulled out a chair for her and sat on the edge of the desk, one long leg swinging idly. 'How do you think the idea of moving will be received by the people concerned?'

Eleanor thought for a moment, watching what looked like a hand-made shoe moving to and fro just within her vision.

'Principally with relief, I should think,' she said finally, looking up at him. 'Everyone is aware that we haven't been as busy lately. Recession has made itself felt, and I'm sure that some of the junior staff have been feeling a trifle uneasy. I think in the main they'll jump at the idea. Jobs aren't easy to come by.'

He was suddenly still, and looked at her for a long moment.

'Have you thought about it from a personal view-point?'

'You mean my own position?' Eleanor tried to sound unaffected. 'I realise that once Mr Coulter is in command there'll be no place for me. He has a perfectly good secretary of his own.'

He went on looking at her, lids half-closed over eyes which she now noticed irrelevantly were light blue like his father's.

'I really don't know what to do about you, Mrs Hunt. Transplanting a married employee is relatively straightforward when that employee is male. You, however, pose an entirely different problem.'

Eleanor opened her mouth to reply, then closed it again, her eyes falling to her hands.

'There's absolutely no need to be concerned on my behalf, sir.' She rose to her feet. 'As long as you're prepared to give me a reference I'm sure I'll have no trouble in finding another job when the time comes.'

'You won't consider looking for one immediately?' One eyebrow lifted as he stood erect.

'No, sir,' she said with emphasis. 'I have a personal loyalty to the firm, and a certain amount of quite normal integrity. Without overvaluing myself I think you'll need me during this time of reorganisation. I shall leave only when the changeover is complete. If that's in accordance with your wishes, of course.'

He moved swiftly to open the door for her, smiling down at her with the first warmth he had allowed himself to show. Eleanor blinked.

'I appreciate your attitude more than I can say, Mrs Hunt.' The deep voice was infinitely more attractive without its undertone of frost.

Eleanor pulled herself together hurriedly.

'Not at all, sir,' she said quickly, 'it's the least I can do after all the kindness your father has shown me.'

The friendly expression was wiped from the aquiline face as though erased with a cold sponge.

'Quite so,' he said coldly. 'Perhaps you'd be good enough to let me have the record of the meeting by three o'clock, with copies for all those present, also one for my father.'

'Of course, sir.' Eleanor retreated hurriedly into her own office, shutting the door quietly behind her.

It was wrenched open a moment later and James stood in the doorway, glaring at her.

'I asked you to stop calling me "sir". You're not a bloody parlourmaid!' he snarled.

Eleanor sat down at her desk, unperturbed.

'As you wish, Mr Ramsay,' she smiled politely, then pointedly rolled some paper into her typewriter.

'Aren't you going for your lunch?' he asked irascibly, still looming in the doorway.

'Not if you require the lists and the finished report by three Mr Ramsay. It's one-thirty already. I'm quite accustomed to a sandwich while I work.' She began to type swiftly from the notebook alongside her.

With a muffled exclamation he swung round and left, closing the door behind him with exaggerated care. Eleanor grinned as she took a packet of sandwiches from her drawer. Actually the work could be completed easily within an hour, but she had enjoyed playing the martyr. It was just possible he might feel some faint contrition. Just possible.

The pattern of the next couple of weeks was hectic in the extreme. With the added chore of waiting for buses she rarely reached home before seven-thirty each evening, and she seemed hardly to have closed her eyes at night before her alarm clock shocked her into another new day. Mrs Jenkins became daily more anxious. So did Harriet, as Eleanor got home later and later, until on the Friday evening of the second week, when it was eight o'clock before her arrival, Mrs Jenkins was waiting for her as she turned the key in the lock.

'Now look, my dear, you can't keep this up. You're going to make yourself ill.'

'I'm not enjoying it, Mrs J.,' said Eleanor wearily, 'but this is only a temporary phase. Things should be a shade quieter next week.'

'I should hope so!' Mrs Jenkins's kind face was full of concern. 'Now I put a little casserole in your oven upstairs, steak and kidney and mushrooms, and mind you eat it. I expect you've been living on coffee and buns, and that's not a bit of good when you're working all these hours.'

'Mrs J., darling, you're an angel!' Eleanor kissed her cheek.

'Go on with *you*!' Her landlady flushed with pleasure. 'You go and put your feet up—oh, and ring Mrs Lord. She's rung twice already this evening.'

Eleanor went slowly up the stairs and took off her coat, her empty stomach rumbling as she sniffed at the savoury smell coming from the kitchen. Then she picked up the phone and dialled Harriet's number.

'Dr Lord,' said the calm voice of her brother-in-law.

'Hello, Richard, it's Eleanor. If you're on call I'll ring off.'

'No, not tonight—however, as the doctor in the family, might I enquire if this is the hour you normally return from work?'

'Don't you start!' sighed Eleanor. 'I've already had my landlady on the warpath and Harriet prophesying dire things about my ultimate fate down the wires every evening. Honestly, love, it's unbelievable at work at the moment—constant turmoil, and likely to stay that way until the changeover is completely organised. I expect Harriet told you all about the new man at the top?'

'Ad nauseam. However, turmoil or not, El, you're going to have to shorten your working day or there *will* be dire results. Harriet is fizzing with frustration at my elbow; I'll hand you over.'

Her sister's voice was indignant.

'Eleanor, do you intend to kill yourself?'

'Shan't have to,' said Eleanor flippantly, 'James Ramsay is doing a fairly good job on that score without any help from me.'

'Someone will have to do something about him,' said Harriet darkly. 'What's the matter with him? Is everyone working these crazy hours, while all this hullabaloo is going on?'

'No, just the master and me. I think it's some kind of endurance test to see if I'll give in and beg for mercy. Fat chance!'

'Now, Eleanor,' Harriet began heatedly, 'you're not to be pigheaded. Tell him to stuff his job.'

'Don't be so inelegant, Harriet—what an example to your sons! I presume your daughter is stashed away for the night?'

'Yes, she is, but don't change the subject. You must ease up a bit. Anyway, love, Richard will be over to fetch you in the morning after surgery.'

Eleanor braced herself.

'Now don't explode, Harriet, but I'm working in the morning.'

'Eleanor! Not after the fortnight you've had!'

'Even so. And Harriet, please don't misunderstand,

but I'd rather stay here in the flat again this weekend.'

To Eleanor's surprise Harriet was quiet for a moment.

'You're just done in, aren't you, darling?' The voice on the line was so full of love and concern that Eleanor swallowed resolutely before answering.

'After I come home tomorrow I'm just going to wallow again, Harriet. There's a novel I started last weekend, I shall watch some television, and I probably shan't even get dressed at all on Sunday. I promise to cook myself proper meals, though. I thought I'd get that in before you do.'

'All right, love, I know my mob aren't very restful,' said Harriet, 'but I'll hold you to next weekend, as we're having a little gathering on Saturday evening. Just a few of the neighbours and the other doctors, and Richard has a new trainee. I thought I'd better entertain him. You can come and be nice to him in case he's lonely.'

Eleanor laughed.

'You're incorrigible, Harriet, you never give up, do you? Love to the boys, a kiss to my baby girl, and I'll give you a ring on Sunday evening.'

The weekend was spent just as Eleanor planned. She shopped on the way home from the office on Saturday, and didn't stir outside the house again until it was time to leave for work on Monday morning.

As she sat in the bus on the way into town she wondered what this week would bring. It could hardly be more hectic than the preceding ones, at least she hoped not. It was a gloomy, wet morning, and she hurried from the bus stop under her gay red umbrella, her trenchcoat belted tightly against a cold, eddying wind, her feet trying to avoid the puddles that threatened her black leather boots.

Eleanor was half an hour early, but even so James was already at his desk when she took in the mail.

'Good morning, Mrs Hunt.' He was brisk. 'Have you a list of today's interviews, please?'

'Good morning, Mr Ramsay. I left it in your engagement diary.'

'Thank you. I expect to be finished with these by the end of the morning. This afternoon I shall want a meeting of the usual group of people to report on my conclusions and the responses of the various candidates. You will please sit in and record.'

'Yes, Mr Ramsay.'

'I shall leave today's mail until after the meeting.' The blue eyes were watchful.

Eleanor was unmoved.

'Very well, Mr Ramsay. Is that all for the time being?'

At his curt nod she returned to her office and sat for a moment, fists clenched and breathing deeply. Yes, Mr Ramsay, no, Mr Ramsay, three bags full, Mr Ramsay, she thought mutinously. He could easily have given her the dictation now, there was a full hour before the first interview. She gritted her teeth, then rang the typing pool to fetch their share of the day's mail.

The day progressed at the rate that had become the norm since James Ramsay's advent. A steady stream of young men passed into the head office with anxious faces, to emerge with expressions varying from relief to elation. Long-distance calls came in at regular intervals, mainly from Saudi Arabia and Brazil, each one holding up the progress of the day's programme. The meeting scheduled for two o'clock finally started at three-fifteen and finished at five-thirty.

'Right,' said James, an unholy expression glinting in

his eyes, 'ready to make a start on the mail now, Mrs Hunt?'

'Yes, Mr Ramsay.' Eleanor kept her voice colourless with an effort. Her pencil had been flying over the pages of her shorthand notebook practically non-stop for the past two hours at the meeting. Now, by the look of the pile in front of him, her new boss was likely to be dictating for another hour at the very minimum. Pig! she thought childishly.

She fetched fresh pencils and a new notebook, and was immediately plunged into the world of feasibility estimates and tenders for various contracts, until by seven o'clock, just as she felt neither her brain nor her hand could function co-ordinately any longer, he came to a halt.

'I think we'll call it a day, Mrs Hunt.'

'Yes, Mr Ramsay,' she said wearily. 'Goodnight.'

'Just a moment, sit down again.' He sat relaxed in the big leather chair, rolling a fountain pen between his fingers, considering her with a blue detached gaze.

Eleanor waited.

'Don't these irregular hours play havoc with your—er—domestic arrangements, Mrs Hunt?'

'Not in the slightest,' said Eleanor distantly, preparing to depart.

'I realise,' he went on relentlessly, 'I've been somewhat remiss these past two weeks—I gather my father used to take you to dinner when he worked you too much. Apparently your husband appears to have been quite happy about the arrangement. Perhaps you'd allow me the same privilege this evening—there's the telephone if you need to ring home to explain.' His eyes held hers with challenge.

Eleanor returned his look with acute dislike.

'Mr Ramsay, you know your father much better than

I do. You are, I'm sure, well aware of his particular brand of humour. The small detail he omitted about the dinners you mention was their precise location. When there was a rush on your mother would insist on my coming home with your father to have dinner with them in case I was too tired to cook for myself. You must know better than anyone that she's the kindest person imaginable, and she'd worry in case I wasn't eating properly.' There was an odd little silence while Eleanor paused to damp down the bright blaze of anger that was in danger of getting out of hand. 'As for my husband, Mr Ramsay, he's tragically not in a position either to object or to approve. He died six years ago.'

In a daze of weariness and white-faced fury, she felt a tear trickle down her cheek as she rose hastily and turned blindly for the door, unaware of the expression on James's face as he sprang out of his chair. As she was groping for the door handle she felt his hand on her arm.

She looked pointedly at the hand on her sleeve until he removed it.

'Mrs Hunt—Eleanor, please don't cry.' For the first time since he'd arrived his voice was without the distant chill undertone.

'Am I crying?' Eleanor was surprised. 'I thought I'd forgotten how. It's sheer rage, you know, also possibly I'm a little tired, I suppose. I'd like to go home now, unless you want any of this typed before I leave.'

'For God's sake, don't turn the knife! I feel low enough as it is.' James raked his hand through his thick black hair distractedly. 'Why on earth didn't you tell me you were a widow?'

'What possible interest could it have had for you?' Eleanor was faintly surprised. 'Besides, I hate the word. To some men it has obvious connotations. If one is young, and even moderately presentable, they add the word "merry" and think one is in need of immediate, if transient, physical consolation. So I never willingly bring the subject up.'

He remained where he was, still barring her way. Eleanor glanced up at him incuriously, unprepared for his swift movement as he suddenly took her in his arms and held her closely against him. Astonished, affronted and dazed by weariness, she leaned momentarily off balance against his hard muscular body, long enough for his fingers to turn up her face to his as his mouth came down on hers. She struggled frantically; she bit his bottom lip and lashed out with one high-heeled boot, catching James in the shin and effectively loosening his hold. She tore herself out of his arms and stood with breasts heaving as she glared into the rueful face still far too near her own.

'I've worked all day and every day for you since you arrived,' she spat at him bitterly. 'This I am paid for. I won't stand for being mauled! You see how right I was? The moment I mentioned the word "widow" you ran true to form!'

James was busy stanching the flow of blood from his mouth with his handkerchief.

'You make your point with considerable emphasis,' he said wryly. 'My sole intention was comfort. What followed was quite involuntary, I assure you, just a natural progression. I apologise humbly for my cave-man tactics, also for my absurd suspicions about you and my father. I think my vision has been distorted ever since I met you.' He paused, reddening slightly, to Eleanor's fascination. 'I apologise even more humbly for what I said about your husband; I can only plead ignorance. For some odd reason of his own Father saw fit to keep me in the dark. You can take satisfaction in 'the fact that you've damn near crippled me, and I doubt if I'll be able to eat dinner tonight!'

'I'm sorry for kicking you, at least, Mr Ramsay,' said Eleanor stiffly.

'Please call me James.'

'Certainly not!' she snapped. 'Now, if you don't mind, I really would like to go home. I have a great deal to get through tomorrow.'

'Eleanor,' James caught her hand, 'please don't cringe. I'm not going to "maul" you again. I just want you to say I'm forgiven for being such a swine to you these past couple of weeks. I know you'll find it hard to believe, but I rather think it's all been due to jealousy.'

Eleanor resolutely ignored the last.

'Oh, all right,' she said irritably, 'if it will make any difference you're forgiven, but I really must go now or I'll miss my bus.'

'I'll take you home,' he said quickly. 'Go and fetch your coat.'

She looked up at him suspiciously, brushing back a straying strand of hair from her forehead. This persuasive man, with the cajoling expression in the ice-blue eyes, was hardly recognisable as the slavedriving tyrant of the past two weeks.

'Please, Eleanor,' he said softly, 'be kind and give me the chance to make up just a little for being such a lout.'

She smiled, then shrugged.

'Very well, but only because I'm tired.'

He waited while she collected her belongings, then they went down the deserted staircase and out through the back entrance of the building into the car park. They made their way through the puddles to James's car, which gleamed in solitary state by the light of the street lamp. Eleanor gazed at the car with respect as she sank into its plush interior.

'A Porsche, no less—how impressive!'

'Upholds the image,' he said briefly as he backed out into Westgate Street. 'Where do you live?'

'Mill Crescent, near the park.'

The short journey was accomplished in a reasonably friendly silence until he drew up outside No. 18.

'Thank you,' said Eleanor brightly, 'that was certainly a lot swifter than my bus ride. How do I unfasten this thing?'

James leaned over, released both her safety belt and the catch on the door, but stayed leaning over her. He looked down into the pale blur of her upturned face.

'Will you bite and kick if I kiss you goodnight just once, very chastely?'

Eleanor knew she should protest, push him away, but she was silent as his face came down until his lips were a mere breath away. He remained motionless for a moment, then his mouth came down gently on her own and his arms slid gently around her. All will to move left Eleanor as his hold tightened and his mouth began to roam over hers in little nibbling kisses, each one a little longer and insistent than the last. Eleanor began to tremble as he became more urgent, and instantly he lifted his head.

'Don't be afraid, Eleanor,' he whispered, 'I won't hurt you.'

His mouth returned to hers, and in triumph he felt her lips part, responding to his coaxing hesitantly at first, then answering his demand so sweetly that his embrace became more intense, and she struggled instinctively. He released her instantly, bending his head to kiss the tip of her nose, then got out of the car to open her door.

'Goodnight, Eleanor, I'll see you in the morning.'

'Goodnight.' Eleanor went swiftly up the garden path without looking back. She had let herself in and was sitting slumped on her settee before she heard the Porsche's powerful engine purr silently down Mill Crescent.

She sat staring into space, hardly able to credit the events of the past hour. I don't dislike him at all, she thought suddenly; I didn't really even in the beginning. Resolutely she began preparing something to eat, deciding to rethink her whole attitude to James Ramsay. Cool, calm and friendly, she thought, slicing tomatoes, that's the attitude. No point in his thinking she was available for a bit of frivolous slap and tickle whenever he was in the mood. Somehow, though, his lovemaking had seemed quite the reverse of frivolous. Stop that right now, my girl, she instructed herself severely, and took her tray into the sitting room to watch a television serial while she ate.

# CHAPTER THREE

When Eleanor woke early next morning her spirits sank. Sheets of rain were streaming down the window, and for the first time since the car had gone she wished she was driving into town. It was also definitely colder, and she shivered as she looked through her wardrobe for something warm to wear. Dressed in claret-coloured sweater and matching pleated skirt she felt decidedly better as she listened to the inane jokes of the morning disc jockey and ate her toast. Collecting raincoat and umbrella, she crept quietly down the stairs, trying not to disturb Mrs Jenkins.

Eleanor gasped as the wind and rain met her with a blast when she opened the door. She fled down the garden path, her trenchcoat collar high round her face and her umbrella well down over her head. She was on the pavement before she saw the long black car at the kerb, and realised that James Ramsay was holding open the passenger door for her.

She subsided thankfully into the low seat, gasping for breath as she looked questioningly at the man beside her. He was wearing a dark brown suit, with a cream silk shirt emphasising the tan of his face, and looked even more attractive than usual.

'Good morning.' His voice was grave as he started the car, but his face was alight with amusement.

'Good morning, yourself,' returned Eleanor. 'Just passing?'

'No. My policy is always to be honest. As it was such a foul morning I thought it would be a good idea to collect you. Until last night I had no idea you came by public transport.'

'A lot of ordinary mortals do, you know,' said Eleanor, smiling sideways at him. 'Actually it's a very recent arrangement. My ancient little car expired of old age a fortnight ago, and I don't feel inclined to go in for another one. It's quite restful travelling by bus—you should try it.'

James turned an apologetic look in her direction.

'It really added to my amour propre last night when I realised that you were having to catch a bus on top of all those late hours I'd been inflicting on you. I had dinner with my parents last night, and you should have heard my mother on the subject; she fairly flayed me alive for victimising Dad's little paragon!'

'I had begun to thaw.' Eleanor was frosty. 'Integrity or not, if you use that word once more I shall resign on the spot!'

James raised one long hand from the steering wheel in apology.

'Sorry! I had an idea it didn't go down well with you. In which case you may be happy to learn that I'm leaving you in peace for the rest of the week. I'm needed in London for a few days, so I'll just skim through the morning mail and I'll be off. Perhaps I could just have the report on yesterday's meeting before I go. I want to be away by eleven.'

'Yes, of course,' said Eleanor absently, surprised to find the prospect of his absence less welcome than he supposed. 'By the way, how did you know what time to pick me up this morning?'

He chuckled.

'I didn't. I'd been hanging round for about ten minutes.'

She frowned.

'I'm uneasy. After the sub-zero atmosphere of the last couple of weeks, I find all this—er—bonhomie a little suspect. Are you lulling me into a false sense of security?'

James turned into the car park and brought the Porsche to a halt. He turned in his seat and put a hand on Eleanor's arm as she wrestled with the intricacies of the seat-belt.

'Don't rush off for a moment, Eleanor, we're early. Before the daily holocaust begins I want to abase myself once more for my behaviour in general, and the overwork in particular. Try to understand that as the first sight I had of you was in my father's arms, for various reasons I was not over-pleased. To bring my cup to overflowing, you politely put me in the right about your being married, or so I thought. I went home that night far from pleased with life. Could you bring yourself to spend an evening with me, and perhaps tell me a little about yourself? When I calmed down and gave it some thought it hit me between the eyes. If your husband died six years ago, you were practically a baby at the time.'

Eleanor was quiet for some time, staring out at the rain streaming down the windscreen. Finally she turned to look at him.

'There's not really very much to tell, but if you want to hear it I don't mind telling my life-story.'

'I really would like to hear it.' James picked up her hand. 'I'll be back on Saturday morning. Have dinner with me in the evening.'

'I'm very sorry, James, but I already have something on.'

He put her hand back on her knee and said bleakly.

'Of course—stupid of me. After six years there must be someone else who has a call on your time.' He looked sideways at her sharply as Eleanor chuckled.

'You're so right! But the person, or rather persons, in question are my sister, her G.P. husband, three small sons and a baby daughter. Harriet leaves me to my own devices during the week, on the strict understanding that I spend most weekends with them. They live out at Tollmarston, on the way to Coventry.'

James turned her face towards him with a long finger and looked down at her intently.

'There's no man at all in your life?'

Eleanor coloured as those searching blue eyes met her own, but she met his look squarely.

'Apart from the four I've just mentioned, none at all.'

'Would your sister let you off for just one Saturday?'

'Of course she would, I'm a free agent, but the last two weekends I was too fagged to want anything but to lie around like a dead thing completely on my own, so I stayed in the flat. I'd been worked to death at the office, you know.' She grinned at his look of contrition. 'This weekend she has a few people in for one of her small gatherings, and I usually give a hand with the food, put Victoria to bed—that sort of thing.' Eleanor hesitated. 'James?'

'Yes?' He shot a sideways look at her.

'Would you like to come? Harriet and Richard would be delighted, they're a very hospitable pair. Unless, of course, you find that sort of thing a bore. I mean, please don't hesitate to say no if you'd rather not.'

'I'll be there whenever you say,' James was swift to interrupt. 'What's the address, and the name of my unsuspecting hosts?'

'Hedgerows, Stoney Lane, Tollmarston—Dr Richard Lord. The house is the third on the left and

has one of those Victorian lamp-posts in the garden.'
Eleanor was rather taken aback by his prompt reaction.

James scribbled in a small black notebook and put it
back in his breast-pocket, then peered out at the rain.

'I suppose you realise, Mrs Hunt, that most of the
staff have now arrived and are burning with curiosity
as to why you're in my car first thing in the morning.
Your reputation is now irretrievably damaged. Here,
let me hold that umbrella over you while you get out.
God, what a morning!'

Eleanor slid out of the car hurriedly.

'Perhaps I'd better go in alone.'

'Ashamed to be seen with me, no doubt.' He took
her elbow in a relentless grip and marched her through
the back door of the building.

At the reception desk Louise's face was a picture as
she saw them come in together.

'Good morning, Eleanor, Mr Ramsay.' Her eyes
were wide.

'Morning, Louise,' said James cheerfully, still retaining his grip on Eleanor's unwilling arm. 'Nothing
in on the Telex yet?'

'No, sir, but Mr Coulter would like a word with you
when you can.'

James nodded and started up the stairs with
Eleanor.

'Let me go!' she muttered.

His blue eyes were alight with laughter as they
stopped on the landing.

'Embarrassed?'

'Extremely. I'm not used to being the centre of
attention, and I don't particularly want to make a
beginning right now.'

'Temper, temper,' he said benignly, taking off his

leather trenchcoat. 'Go and take your raincoat off, then bring in all the really urgent things and we'll get cracking.'

'Yes, sir,' said Eleanor, escaping hurriedly.

By eleven-thirty she had finished the report and a large proportion of the previous day's letters, which James signed while he drank his coffee.

'You can cope with all the rest yourself,' he said, flicking through the letters quickly. 'You alter things around anyway.'

'Only when you've repeated yourself.' Eleanor was defensive.

'All right, all right, the finished version is always highly polished, but then it should be, Miss Cleversticks, you're the one with the English degree, after all.' James stood up and stretched. 'Well, I'd better be off. I'm confident you have more than enough to occupy you for the next couple of days, Eleanor.'

'I'm a bit behind with the more routine stuff,' she admitted, 'I'll be happier when I've caught up.'

He wagged a finger at her as he came round the desk.

'Home at five every afternoon, in bed at nine, and don't overdo things. There's some built-in shadow under your eyes, as well as the stuff you put on the lids.'

'How kind,' said Eleanor demurely. 'In other words, you mean I look like a hag.'

James pulled her up out of her chair and held her firmly by the shoulders.

'Less of the wilful misunderstanding, Eleanor Hunt. What I actually do mean is something I'll go into when there's more time—and more opportunity.'

Eleanor disengaged herself swiftly and handed him his leather coat and briefcase.

'Drive carefully. It's still raining heavily, there's bound to be a lot of spray on the motorway.'

'You said that as if you meant it,' he said, slinging his coat round his shoulders.

'Of course I do. That's a powerful piece of machinery you drive, so don't go mad on the M1.'

James turned in the doorway.

'I'll be with you on Saturday night, Eleanor. How would your sister expect me to be dressed?'

'Oh, the men are fairly casual and the women anything from glamorous to weird. You'll be welcome however you come.'

'Will I, Eleanor?' He looked at her very directly, the blue eyes intent.

Eleanor's dark ones were unwavering on his as she nodded.

He smiled suddenly and was gone, leaving Eleanor undecided whether she was relieved or bereft by his departure.

After two days of comparative peace, catching up on her routine, having lunch with Frances again, and sleeping like the dead each night, Eleanor felt considerably more like herself.

She strolled back after lunch with Frances on the Friday afternoon, enjoying some anaemic November sunshine. The latter suddenly brought up a subject that had been occupying a large part of Eleanor's mind for the past two weeks.

'There's something that really bothers me, Eleanor. It seems hardly fair that the new set-up is going to phase you out of a job completely.'

'Don't worry, I'm sure to find another job without too much difficulty, I'm quite well qualified, and the Ramsays are sure to give me a good recommendation.'

Frances's face was troubled.

'Isn't there a niche for you in London?'

Eleanor laughed gaily.

'Good heavens, no, that's the last place I want to go. I'm perfectly happy in my cosy little retreat here. I must say I'm looking forward to seeing Harriet this weekend. Instead of bringing Richard out in the morning I'll get up early and catch a bus.'

'Of course, no transport—I'd forgotten about the car. Why not go this evening?'

'I hadn't thought to, but there's no reason why not, I suppose. Why?'

'I'm driving into Coventry to pick up Colin from the London train about seven. I could pick you up and drop you off at Harriet's on my way.'

'Lovely. Thanks a lot, Fran—about sixish, then.'

Eleanor worked through the afternoon with a light heart, and was finished by three-thirty. She went along to France's office and put her head round the door.

'I'm off now, taking my time in lieu to do a bit of shampooing.'

Frances turned from the filing cabinet, a smile on her face.

'That lot needs a fair drying time. Why don't you have it cut?'

'It's easier this way. Anyway, I'm nervous of being chopped and frizzed. I only wish I had Harriet's curls.' Eleanor thrust a hand over the heavy coil ruefully. 'See you later, and thanks again.'

She went back to make sure James's office was ship-shape for Monday. Odd how soon it had become 'James's office', she thought, and returned to her own room just as her telephone rang.

The deep voice on the line accelerated her pulse.

'Why haven't you gone home, Eleanor? I told you to

take it easy until I get back.' James's voice was stern.

'If I had I wouldn't be talking to you now,' she pointed out reasonably. 'Is there something you want me to do for you?'

'Perhaps I could take you up on that tomorrow night!' She could picture his teasing smile clearly. 'In the meantime I just thought I'd remind you that we have a date, of sorts at least, in case it had slipped your mind.'

'No, I hadn't forgotten.'

'Good; but I may be a little later than planned, as there's still quite a bit to clear up here tomorrow. Is all well with you?'

'Perfectly, thank you.'

'Then go home—now. That's not a request, it's an order.'

Eleanor laughed softly.

'Your wish is my command, sir. I'm on my way.'

'Until tomorrow then. *Ciao*.'

Eleanor left the building warmed by a feeling of anticipation. On her way to the bus stop she bought a quantity of sweets and several comics for the boys, also a soft velvet ball for the baby.

She sang in the bathroom all through the shampooing session, and sat with a mug of coffee while she dried her hair with an electric brush. The lengthy process completed, she plaited the bright hair into a thick shiny rope and dressed in black cord jeans and pale yellow sweater and tugged on black knee-length boots. She packed underwear and night things in her weekend bag, then looked through her wardrobe for something to wear to the party. None of the contents appealed in the slightest. With sudden decision she closed the wardrobe, shut her case and went downstairs to say goodbye to Mrs Jenkins.

Frances duly collected her and dropped her at the end of Stoney Lane. She stuck her face out of the window and yelled at Eleanor.

'You should wear that plait hanging down your back more often. It does things for you!'

Eleanor waved her off, smiling, and set off down the road towards Hedgerows and Harriet. She had decided not to ring beforehand, hoping the surprise would be welcome. She made her way through the large garden towards the rambling pre-war house built of Cotswold stone. She pressed the bell alongside the heavy oak door with its wrought-iron hinges, and waited expectantly. The door was opened by eight-year-old Edward, whose face lit up as he hurled himself at her.

'Auntie El, we thought you were coming tomorrow!'

He was instantly joined by his two small brothers and two vociferous large Labradors, all of whom surrounded her with noise, the dogs barking and the boys talking nineteen to the dozen as they pulled her into the hall, Edward importantly taking charge of her case.

Harriet came running down the stairs, arms outstretched.

'Eleanor! What a super surprise, how did you get here?'

'Frances Marshall offered me a lift, so I came this evening instead of tomorrow. Not putting you out, am I?'

'How on earth could you do that, stupid? You owe us a bit of extra time anyway, after your defection the last two weekends!'

They all trooped into the lounge, where Eleanor was installed on the largest settee, with a nephew on either side and one in her lap, and dogs all over her feet. She sighed blissfully as Harriet handed her a glass of sherry.

'It seems ages since I was here, not just weeks. I've missed you all. Where's Vicky?'

'In bed. I'd have kept her up if I'd known you were coming tonight, but I'm glad I didn't really; much nicer to be surprised.'

Harriet drew back, her head on one side, looking at Eleanor consideringly.

'You look different.'

'I couldn't be bothered to put my hair up after I washed it—I expect it's the juvenile plait.'

'Possibly.' Harriet was unconvinced. 'You look—let me see, blooming, I think.'

Eleanor laughed, feeling oddly selfconscious.

'The effects of the new shampoo, definitely guaranteed to make one look like a new woman—what is it, David?'

The four-year-old on her knee was regarding her with expectant eyes as he tugged on her plait to attract her attention.

Eleanor pretended not to understand.

'I wonder what you want, David Lord.'

'Didn't you bring us anyfing, Auntie El?' he asked anxiously.

'You're not supposed to ask,' said Charles reprovingly, full of the authority of three years' seniority.

Eleanor relented and directed Edward to her case. He brought it over and opened it on the floor. The comics and sweets were shared out and instant peace reigned, even Juno and Sophie getting a sweet or two.

'Come on,' said Harriet, 'let's install you upstairs. Boys, you can watch television for a bit, no fighting, and let me know when Daddy arrives.'

Eleanor looked around her contentedly as they went upstairs. Harriet's home was a mélange of old and new, with deep shaggy bronze-coloured carpet providing a background for chintz-covered settees, velvet chairs, the glint of brass and copper and bowls of flowers everywhere. She breathed deeply, taking in the indefinable smell of home that was compounded of well-polished furniture, fresh flowers and the aroma of good home cooking.

Harriet dumped the suitcase on the bed in the spare bedroom and sat down beside it, looking at Eleanor expectantly.

'Well, how are things at the salt-mines? You appear to have survived remarkably well, all things considered.'

'Actually, things are a bit quieter now. James has been in London for two days and I've been able to relax a bit.'

Harriet's eyebrows disappeared practically into her hair.

'James? Are you on first name terms now? When I spoke to you last you weren't exactly chummy.'

Eleanor fiddled with her hair in the dressing table mirror for a moment, then said casually:

'Do you mind having another guest tomorrow night, Harriet?'

Harriet shot to her feet, eyes aglow.

'You've invited someone, darling? Of course I don't mind. Who is it?'

'James Ramsay. Really, Harriet, do close your mouth, you're gaping!'

'James Ramsay?' repeated Harriet in amazement. 'But I thought it was daggers drawn between you, and he thought you were a popsie on the make for his father!'

'Where do you get some of your vulgar expressions? Actually he now knows I'm not a popsie, as you so elegantly put it, also that I no longer have a husband. In fact, he's quite remorseful about being so—well, so difficult in the beginning.'

'Difficult!' snorted Harriet, beginning to unpack the suitcase. 'I think that's a bit of an understatement, Eleanor. By the way, as a matter of interest, there are no clothes in here, only your nightie and underwear. We are having a party tomorrow, you know.'

'If Richard isn't on in the morning, I thought perhaps you could spare an hour to come to Coventry. I want something to wear.' Eleanor looked a little sheepish. 'I'm a bit tired of my plain jane stuff.'

Harriet beamed.

'No, he isn't, and yes, I will. I adore spending other people's money.' She stopped suddenly, looking curiously at Eleanor. 'Is this because James Ramsay is coming tomorrow night?'

'Yes,' said Eleanor simply, 'I rather think it is.'

'It's all right, El, is it?' said Harriet anxiously. 'I mean, you won't get hurt, or anything.'

'Not even "anything", I shouldn't think. I'm a big girl now, and I just want something new. For the first time since Nick died I have a date I made myself. Actually James wanted to take me out to dinner on Saturday; to make amends, I think, so as I didn't want to revert to hostilities I thought he might like to come here. He certainly accepted with alacrity.'

'I should think so, too,' said Harriet, laughing. 'Invitations to the Lords' soirées are hard to come by. That sounds vaguely blasphemous somehow, doesn't it? Oh, goody, from the racket downstairs that must be Richard.'

Eleanor followed slightly more slowly as her sister flew down the stairs to kiss her large, fair-haired husband with enthusiasm.

'Hello, darling, isn't it lovely, Eleanor's come tonight instead of tomorrow, and you don't mind keeping an eye on the boys in the morning, she needs to go to Coventry in the morning to buy something new and she's invited James Ramsay to our do and——'

'Yes to everything,' interrupted Richard, smiling down at her indulgently. He turned and gave Eleanor a hug, then inspected her mock-professionally, a twinkle in his deceptively lazy grey eyes. 'You're supposed to be all pale, wan and pathetic, from this tale of woe I've been getting from Harriet in serial form most nights,' he said teasingly, 'but in that get-up, with that braid hanging down your back, you look like a fifteen-year-old, and a sexy one at that!'

Eleanor went scarlet, much to the others' amusement, and hastily volunteered to put David to bed and read him his story. She gave him a piggyback up the stairs, calling down to Harriet:

'It hasn't embarrassed the dinner situation, having to stretch to another plateful?'

'Of course not; a very elastic casserole tonight. I'll throw on extra peas and add a potato to the pan. You don't eat much anyway.'

'Don't count on that,' said Eleanor. 'Hang on, David, you're subsiding a bit. Actually, Harriet, I'm quite hungry.'

The other two looked at each other with raised eyebrows as Eleanor disappeared with her burden.

'What's all this about her new boss coming tomorrow night?' said Richard, relishing his first sherry of the day. 'I thought he wasn't exactly high on her popularity list.'

'Things appear to have changed somewhat this week, love. I only hope . . .' Harriet's voice trailed away and she looked up at him anxiously.

Her husband put an arm round her and kissed her cheek.

'You can't protect her from everything, Harriet. Eleanor is a mature, sensible girl. And what's more he can't have his evil way with her when he takes her home as she's staying here. Now how about that dinner—I'm ravenous!'

# CHAPTER FOUR

ELEANOR woke early next morning and tiptoed into the room next door to find eight-month-old Victoria sitting up in her cot, arms held up in entreaty.

'All right, my charmer,' said Eleanor, scooping her up, 'I'll get you dressed and we'll have breakfast together.'

She enjoyed coping with the warm, wriggling little body, and quickly had Vicky in stretch-towelling dungarees and sweater, ready for her breakfast in the sunny kitchen with its pine cupboards, yellow gingham curtains and windowsills crowded with potted plants.

'What would you care for, chicken?' Eleanor nuzzled the baby's neck before putting her into her high-chair. 'How about porridge followed by boiled egg and soldiers?'

'Great!' Harriet was yawning widely as she came into the kitchen. 'Make that for three. How are you this morning, Auntie?'

'Fine, thanks, I slept like a top. You put the coffee on and I'll do the rest.'

Working companionably together, they were soon eating their meal, taking turns to pop spoonfuls into Vicky's waiting open mouth.

'We'll take her with us, Eleanor, she's no trouble, and if we go really early we can park near this fabulous shop I've found.'

'Fabulous prices too, no doubt.'

'You get what you pay for, love. Besides, I don't recall your buying anything partyish for ages. What did you have in mind?' Harriet's eyes gleamed over her coffee-cup.

'You know what I fancy, Harriet? Something mad and impractical. I don't know precisely what, but something slinky and sophisticated. I've been getting a bit too plain and tailored lately.'

Harriet sprang up and began washing dishes quickly.

'Let's get cracking, then, I'm sure Honorine will have something to take your fancy. I don't think she's French really, it's just the image she likes to project, but she certainly has taste.'

They were soon on their way to Coventry in Harriet's red Mini, the baby gurgling contentedly in her car seat in the back.

'James has a Porsche,' remarked Eleanor casually, as they neared the city.

'Very smooth! Have you been in it?'

'He gave me a lift home the other night, actually, and then he came and picked me up and took me into work next morning because the weather was so filthy.'

Harriet's face was so expressive in her struggle to look unsurprised that Eleanor roared with laughter.

'Honestly, Eleanor,' Harriet was indignant, 'you didn't say a word about that last night, you meanie! The state of affairs has changed rather radically from last week, by the sound of it.'

'He's rather charming when he's not being sarcastic. In fact I now see why he used to be a target for all the unmarried ladies; possibly married ones too, for all I know.'

Harriet frowned as she slowed down to negotiate the heavier volume of traffic.

'Have you fallen for him, Eleanor?' she said bluntly.

'No. But I begin to see how easy it might be to do

so. Anyway, I've only asked him to your party; I can hardly come to grief in a room full of people. I think he's keen to make reparation for his suspicions about me—and with his father, of all people!'

'Hm.' Harriet was noncommittal. 'Nevertheless we may as well equip you with some armour. A few fine feathers make splendid moral support.'

When they arrived at the boutique Eleanor began to have cold feet when she saw how exclusive-looking the smart little shop looked.

'How much is this little encounter going to set me back, Harriet? It looks a bit rarefied.'

'Money well spent.' Harriet was firm. 'I bought the dress I'm wearing tonight here last week. Richard thinks I look fantastic in it.'

'Richard thinks you look fascinating in anything, so that's nothing to go by.'

Harriet pushed her daughter's carriage into the perfumed interior of the elegant little shop, leaving Eleanor to bring up the rear. She greeted the austere woman in a starkly plain black dress who came forward to meet them.

'Madame Honorine, good morning. I know you don't mind my bringing my baby; she's fast asleep, actually. This is my sister, Mrs Hunt, and she wants something special.'

'Mrs Lord—a pleasure to see you again. How do you do, Mrs Hunt, please tell me what you have in mind, I'm sure I shall be able to show you something that will please.'

Eleanor was hesitant.

'Just a short dress, possibly black, nothing very complicated—I don't sound very decisive, I'm afraid.'

The woman looked at her appraisingly.

'Size ten, I think?'

Eleanor nodded.

An hour later they emerged, Harriet triumphant and Eleanor slightly dazed. Honorine had tactfully pointed out that garnet-coloured pure silk would look much better against Eleanor's olive skin than black. The dress she produced was very slim and straight, with shoe-string shoulder straps and a matching short jacket made entirely of sequins in the same shade of dull dark red.

'Can you spare a few more minutes, Harriet, I'll need new sandals to go with the dress.' Eleanor was by this time bereft of caution.

Harriet assented rapturously, and in a short while they were back in the car, Eleanor with her arms full of packages. Apart from fragile black ankle-strap sandals there was a strapless wisp of black lace bra to go under the dress, new perfume and a lipstick in the same dark red as the dress.

As they drove home Eleanor was beset by doubts.

'You realise I'm practically bankrupt, Harriet,' she said ruefully.

'Nonsense! That get-up is worth every last penny. Strange how the dress is so plain and yet so sexy at the same time.'

'Sexy?' Eleanor was startled. 'Do you think it's a bit obvious?'

'For heaven's sake,' snorted Harriet, 'you dress like the prototype of the perfect secretary every day. Surely you're entitled to dazzle once in a while. You can let down that hair—literally too—perhaps wear it in a plait again. It suits you.'

Eleanor had doubts about the last, but by this time they were home. Immediately they were swamped by dogs and boys, and her qualms were lost in the frenzied activity that took up the rest of the day.

After lunch Eleanor sat with Vicky on her knee while the boys played in the garden, and the three adults lingered over their coffee, Harriet animatedly describing the new dress to Richard.

He looked at Eleanor's pensive face enquiringly.

'Cold feet, El?'

'Something like that,' she said ruefully. 'I can't imagine now why I asked him—I'm not given to impulses as a rule. Only oddly enough he seemed a bit hurt when I said I was tied up.'

'Well, don't get in a twist, love,' said Harriet briskly, 'there'll be plenty of people here you can palm him off on to—Althea Smallwood is coming, for a start.'

Eleanor chuckled.

'Althea's a dear really, and at least you can always rely on her to wear something that gives the other guests something to buzz about.'

'She's got two main interests in life, men and horses.' Harriet began to clear away. 'Do you know, she came to my coffee-morning for Save the Children in jeans that were literally encrusted with hay and manure, topped by a much-shrunk sweater with a hole in the sleeve. She'd been up in the night with that mare of hers and came along just as she was. Then at night she's all see-through chiffon, or skin-tight leather and boots. Actually, she's very good-hearted. She just seems such an amazing wife for a consultant.'

'Or indeed anyone,' murmured Richard, grinning as he gave his wife a hand.

'Anyway, Eleanor, you can give James to Althea if you're uptight.'

Harriet's expression was mischievous.

'He's not a pound of tea! James is not precisely the type it's possible to push around.'

*

By six that evening Harriet and Eleanor had prepared all the food between them. Harriet had made a pastry crust, spread it with pâté and mushrooms and wrapped it round a succulent filet of steak, and this splendid creation was now waiting to go into the oven just before the guests were due to arrive. The rest of the food was cold—different quiches, previously baked, a large joint of deliciously rare roast beef, a ham, plenty of accompanying salads and a platter of mixed cheeses.

Eleanor rounded up the boys while Harriet was seeing to the baby.

'You two go in the big bathroom, Edward, Charles,' she suggested, 'I'll take David in Mummy's, then we'll play something quiet after tea while Mummy and Daddy get ready for the party.'

'Snakes and Ladders,' said David firmly.

'We always play that,' grumbled Edward.

'Snakes and Ladders first,' said Eleanor decisively, 'then I put David to bed and you, Charles and I will play Yahtzee.'

Approval gained all round, soon three shiningly clean boys were putting away large quantities of soup and scrambled eggs while Eleanor entertained Vicky with a bit of energetic slip-fielding as the baby continually hurled the velvet ball out of the playpen, accompanied by ecstatic shrieks of laughter.

Eventually it was almost seven before Eleanor began to dress, the two younger children in bed, the other two allowed to watch television until the arrival of the guests.

Eleanor had a quick shower, then put on the dark red silk dress. Zipping it up in front of her bedroom mirror, she looked at herself doubtfully. No one could deny it was a perfect fit; Eleanor hoped the fit was not over-perfect as she strained to see herself from the back. She made up her face with more than usual care, using a little extra blusher and emphasising her wide dark eyes. The new lipstick was perfect and she made a face at herself in the mirror when the final touch was made. Anyone would think this was a Command Performance!

Despite Harriet's advice, Eleanor had no intention of leaving her hair down. She let it fall into two gleaming wings from a centre parting, sweeping the main mass of it up into a knot on the crown of her head. She fastened on her little gold E, sprayed herself with perfume, put on her sandals, added the sequin jacket and took one final look at herself. Well, Eleanor, that's it, she told herself; considering the basic material, that's the best result it's possible to produce.

'Are you ready, darling?' Harried dashed in in a whirl of brick-coloured chiffon printed with splashy black tulips.

'What a superb dress, Harriet—Richard was dead right.'

'Never mind me, love, let's look at you. Turn round.' Harriet was silent for so long Eleanor became restive.

'Do I look odd, or something? Don't just stand there mute!'

Harriet let out a long breath.

'I was trying to find the appropriate word. You look—burnished, as though your skin and hair have caught the glitter in the jacket. I think you ought to go back and give Honorine more money—you had a bargain!'

Eleanor laughed at her sister's extravagance.

'I hope you're not biased.'

Harriet seized her hand and pulled her out of the room.

'Come on, let's go and have a drink and supervise

the music Richard's putting on the record-player. I want something loud and brash with bounce to get us off the ground.'

Richard turned as they went down the stairs to the big softly-lit hall where he had set up his bar.

'What will you drink, girls? I say, Eleanor, you look stunning—no, I mean it. Good thing we're related.'

'Rubbish,' chuckled Eleanor, 'as if you ever saw anyone when Harriet was around! Thank you just the same though, love, and I'll have some white wine, please, which I can stay with all evening.'

Shortly afterwards Harriet shepherded her sons off to bed as the first guests began to arrive, and in a short while the house was filled with music and laughter. Eleanor knew most of the guests, and circulated from group to group offering hors d'oeuvres and keeping an eye on glasses to refill. She was chatting to one of Richard's partners and his wife when she saw her brother-in-law beckoning and excused herself. He was talking to a tall fair young man who turned with alacrity as Eleanor approached. He had a long face with a nose that had obviously been broken at some time and a pair of intelligent brown eyes that held an expression of disbelief as he took Eleanor's hand.

'This is Chris Tate, our new trainee,' said Richard. 'Chris, this is my sister-in-law, Eleanor Hunt. See his glass keeps filled, El, and introduce him around.'

The tall young man led her over to a quiet corner of the L-shaped hall and stood looking down at her, still slightly bemused.

'Sorry if I seem a bit dazed. I've just met Mrs Lord, then before I could recover from the impact Richard produces you. Are there any more gorgeous sisters?'

Eleanor laughed, warmed by his ingenuous smile.

'Just the two of us, I'm afraid.'

He picked up her left hand, then covered his eyes dramatically. 'I might have known you'd be spoken for!' His tone was tragic.

Oh dear, thought Eleanor, here we go.

'I'm a widow, Mr Tate.' Her voice was resigned.

'I suppose I should say I'm sorry, but I'm not—oh Lord, it's not recent, is it?' At the shake of her head he let out a sigh of relief. 'I'm not celebrated for my tact, as you can see. Don't hold it against me.'

'You weren't to know, Mr Tate. Now, who would you like to meet?'

'Please call me Chris. At the moment I'm more than happy to stay exactly where I am, don't cast me off at such short notice.'

Eleanor smiled and held out her glass.

'Perhaps you'd like to refill that with some medium dry white and top up your own. Then you can come back and I'll give the lowdown on who's who.'

He moved off obediently through the gaily chattering crowd and Eleanor glanced down at her watch. Nine already, but no sign of James. She sighed, then smiled brilliantly at Chris as he reappeared with her drink. While she sipped it he asked her about herself and what she did.

Eleanor complied for a while, telling him about her work, then asked him about himself and his background. They chatted amiably for some time, Eleanor telling him about the other guests and local places of interest to visit, discovering a mutual love of the theatre.

'I thought I was supposed to be introducing you to everyone else,' she said eventually.

'I already know the medical ones, and frankly,' he gazed down at her with a decidedly ensnared look, 'you are the one I want to know about. Do you live here, do you have any attachments?'

'Whoa there!' smiled Eleanor. 'Steady on—oh, look—Althea Smallwood has just arrived. Goodness, she does look eye-catching! Her husband, behind her, is the E.N.T. consultant at the General.'

The lady in question, busy embracing Harriet and Richard, was encased in what looked like a pink satin boiler-suit very much unzipped, with gold kid ankle boots and her hair in a wild pale gold frizzled aureole round her head.

Chris Tate turned back to Eleanor in a state of shock.

'I thought consultants' wives wore twin-sets and pearls, or little black dresses.' he said, dazed.

'Althea's the nicest person imaginable, but she is a bit way-out in her taste in clothes.'

'Out of sight, you mean. Your dress is ravishing, though.' He moved closer, blocking her view of the rest of the room. 'May I see you tomorrow; take you to lunch, dinner, or whatever you fancy?'

Eleanor shook her head, smiling.

'Sorry. I'm here for the weekend. Sunday lunch is a ritual with my niece and nephews.'

The brown eyes were determined.

'How about some time during the week?'

Eleanor began to feel hemmed in. He was standing with one arm resting on the wall beside her, altogether too close for comfort.

'Actually,' she said untruthfully, hoping to change the subject, 'I would love another glass of wine.'

'How fortuitous,' said a deep voice, and Chris turned. James stood there, a glass in either hand. 'Your sister said you were drinking white wine, Eleanor.'

Eleanor took the glass from James and handed the empty one to Chris, who was regarding the newcomer without welcome.

'Hello, James, I didn't see you arrive. This is Chris Tate, Richard's new trainee. Chris, this is my boss, James Ramsay.'

The two men murmured polite greetings, then Chris looked from one to the other with rueful comprehension.

'I'll just take your glass back, Eleanor,' he said quietly. 'Thank you for taking pity on me. Nice to meet you, Ramsay.' Then he left to thread his way through the crowd.

Eleanor watched him go sympathetically, hurriedly taking a swallow from her drink as she saw James's speculative eye.

'I didn't see you come in,' said Eleanor, repeating herself, to her annoyance.

'Hardly surprising. Young—Tate, was it?—had you practically obscured from the rest of the room.' James leaned against the wall comfortably. 'Not that I blame him. You look quite incredible.'

'Sounds ambiguous.'

He moved closer, so that their shoulders were touching.

'You know perfectly well what I mean. My hyper-efficient secretary by day is obviously transformed into super-siren after dark. That young man was dazzled, and not just by this glittery thing you're wearing.'

Eleanor surveyed him clinically over the rim of her glass.

'You look a bit different yourself.'

The sober restraint of his daytime office suits had been exchanged for one in string-coloured corduroy worn with a brown silk shirt, the results obvious from the amount of fascinated female glances fluttering in his direction.

'You approve?'

'Oh yes indeed, very macho, absolutely s-sizzling with sex appeal,' she pronounced solemnly. 'All Harriet's friends are seething with curiosity.'

He looked down at her sharply.

'How many glasses of wine have you had?'

'I haven't counted. Are you rudely implying I'm tight?' she said with dignity.

'Not exactly tight, darling,' he murmured, 'but definitely a little mellow.'

Eleanor smiled up at him happily.

'It's rather a pleasant feeling, James, I've never experienced it before. By the way, what did you think of Harriet?'

'A very attractive lady. Your brother-in-law's a lucky man.'

'Do you fancy her, James?'

'Don't be vulgar. I make a point of never fancying other men's wives.' He slid an arm round her waist. 'I'm not above casting an eye at delectable widows, though.'

Eleanor stiffened automatically, then relaxed and smiled up into the teasing blue eyes.

'James, are you flirting with me?'

'I thought no one used that word any more. However, as you asked, yes, Mrs Hunt, I am. Do you object?'

She shook her head and leaned back against his supporting arm.

'What time did you get back?'

James looked at his watch.

'I arrived home about an hour ago, had a shower, threw on the casual party gear requested, and here I am.'

'James! You must be starving. Let's go and collect

some food before the rush.'

'If you'll promise to find us a reasonably secluded spot to eat it.'

'I should be introducing you to people. Althea Smallwood is coming apart at the seams with curiosity.'

'If you mean the blonde in the satin overalls, I met her as I arrived—your sister introduced me to her, and to a couple of medical people, and for the time being that will be perfectly sufficient, thank you. You seem determined to avoid the issue, Eleanor, but let's be quite clear. Apart from the pleasure of meeting your sister and her husband I came tonight for one reason— to see you.'

The last statement was a little direct for Eleanor's taste, and she drained her glass quickly.

'I'd rather you didn't say things like that, James.'

'Why not?' He took her hand in his. 'I believe always in making my position perfectly clear. Now lead me to the dinner table. Apart from being starving myself, something to mop up the excess alcohol might be a good idea for you, too.'

'Nonsense,' said Eleanor firmly. 'I'm just a little happy, that's all.'

They went into the dining-room, where Harriet was presiding over the buffet-table. She looked up in smiling welcome at James.

'You found her, then, Mr Ramsay.'

'I did eventually. A large young man had hidden her in a far corner of the hall, doing his best to keep her to himself. Incidentally, I'd be happy if you'd call me James.'

'Of course; I'm Harriet. Now do have some of my Beef Wellington, and anything else you fancy, and perhaps you'd make sure Eleanor eats something too.

It's no use frowning, Eleanor, you usually run round seeing to everyone else and forget to eat anything yourself. Ah, there's Richard with what looks like some of his full-bodied red.'

They piled their plates obediently with various delicacies, while Eleanor pondered where to take James to consume them. After a small consultation with Richard she took James's hand and led him through a door off the dining-room leading into Richard's study at the back of the house. They sat at the desk like two conspirators.

'This is really being extremely anti-social,' said Eleanor, her mouth inelegantly full.

'Do you mind?'

'Not really.'

'Then let's enjoy it. Not only is this meat pie thing of your sister's superb, but I was getting to the stage where I could have eaten the flower-arrangement in the hall. I was held up in London, had no time for lunch, then eventually had to drive like Ben Hur up the M1. I didn't stop for a snack before coming, like the determined admirer I am.'

Eleanor laid down her knife and fork and drank some wine, looking at James thoughtfully. He paused in his frank enjoyment of his meal and looked across at the big dark eyes that were fixed on him.

'That's an odd look you're giving me, Eleanor.'

'I was just wondering what Harriet's reaction would be to your description of her Beef Wellington as meat pie! Also, to be entirely honest, I was contemplating your amazing volte-face. Last week you were a sarcastic, merciless slavedriver. This week you're transformed into a—a——'

'Fervent admirer, would-be lover, hopeful friend?'

'Your words, not mine. However you like to put it I

find it difficult to adjust from one extreme to the other. For three weeks you were overbearing, hostile and at times downright impossible.'

James put aside his empty plate with a satisfied sigh, leaning back in Richard's swivel chair.

'And what now, Eleanor? Do any of my suggestions appeal to you?'

'I'm not perfectly sure.' Eleanor's eyes dropped before the look in his blue ones, which was so warm it was hard to remember their recent icy expression. 'I'd like to think we could be friends?'

Her look was wide and questioning. He leaned across the desk and took both her hands in his.

'In the beginning,' he said, 'I thought you had a husband. In addition I thought you had my father on a string. Both of these ideas acted like goads which kept me working you and myself to a standstill, as I imagined every hour I kept you late was an hour you were kept from your supposed connubial bliss. Purely and simply, I was as jealous as hell and utterly disgusted with myself into the bargain. It made me a bit difficult to work with, I agree. Jealousy of any sort is a new experience for me. Can you forgive me for all that?'

Eleanor looked at him gravely for a moment, then nodded.

'Thank you.' James settled back in his chair. 'Now do you feel you can tell me how you became a widow so young?'

'Nick was killed on our honeymoon.' Eleanor made an effort to keep her voice unemotional. 'We'd known each other since we were small. He was literally the boy next door, only his house was the largest in the village; the Manor, no less, but it had an adjoining wall on the boundary of the grounds which was our garden wall also at the Vicarage. Are you sure you want to hear all this?'

He nodded, smiling his reassurance.

'Nick went away to prep school and eventually boarding school, but in the holidays we ran wild together. His people were very down on Nick's mixing with the village boys, but as I was the Vicar's daughter I was just about permissible. He taught me to swim in the river—to fish there, too, not that we ever caught much. He showed me how to play tennis, how to ride a bicycle, and even gave me my first few driving lessons.

'He took his degree the year I did A-levels, and was offered a job with a firm of accountants immediately he qualified. He was very bright. Then my father died suddenly just after my results came out and Nick insisted it wasn't worth my going to college, that we should marry at once. It was one of the few times that Harriet and I were at odds; she very much wanted to see me go to college and get my degree first, and then marry Nick afterwards if we were still of the same mind. I was torn in two with wanting to please everyone, but of course I gave in to Nick and, much against Harriet's wishes, and in the teeth of stonewall opposition from his family, we did. Soon afterwards he was killed. Harriet and Richard picked up the pieces, put me back together again, insisted I take up my place in college here. The rest you know.'

James stood up and brought her round the desk, taking her into a light embrace, his arms gentle.

'Growing up must have been sudden and painful, Eleanor.'

She felt a little blurred from the wine, and tired from the emotion of telling her sad little story, that now seemed to have happened to some other girl, a long time ago.

'You know, James, one minute I was a rather clever, harum-scarum creature, skimming through life like a dragonfly. Then overnight childhood was over. Suddenly a new phase began, ruthlessly altered, with no Nick, no father and no home. Perhaps you can realise why I shall always be so indebted to Harriet and Richard. They wanted me to live with them and commute to college, but I dug my heels in and found two other girls to share a flat. It's where I live now, only I can afford to live there alone.' She looked down at her watch. 'James, that's enough of my life story. There's a party going on out there; by now Harriet will have started everyone dancing, otherwise with all these doctors all over the place they'll be talking shop all night.'

Eleanor gave a little sigh, then smiled up at James, blinking almost sleepily.

He smiled back, bending to kiss her swiftly.

'Let's go and tell your sister how much we enjoyed her superb meal, and try and look as though we've been doing the washing up.'

'Really, James, I'm certain you don't know what a dishcloth looks like!'

'I'll have you know I'm an expert—do you think I should offer Harriet my services?'

'Heavens no, she has a dishwasher. Come on, let's go and be sociable. You'll probably have to dance with Althea, and Dr Preston's young daughter was gazing at you with a definite come-on earlier.'

He opened the door for her, muttering into the nape of her neck:

'Not on your life—do you think I'm going to chance your being snapped up by that young doctor? I'm not letting you out of my sight.'

Harriet swooped down on them as they emerged into the hall.

'Drink James? Scotch? Eleanor, lead him to Richard's little bar, then come and join the dancing.'

James complimented her smoothly on the excellence of her meal, and she thanked him prettily, looked at Eleanor for a moment, then flitted off, apparently reassured, and was soon in the midst of a crowd of energetic people moving to the heavy beat of the latest pop record.

James drew Eleanor into the middle of the crowd, and she found he danced in much the same way as he did everything else, with energy and grace. Shortly the music changed to a slow romantic tempo and he slid his arm round her waist, his other hand holding hers flat against his chest. They hardly moved in time to the slow rhythm, their bodies moulded together, relaxed and pliant. Eleanor gave herself up to the music, her body subject to the movements of his, feeling his lips brushing her hair. Suddenly she was jolted out of her trance by a change to louder, faster music. She let James guide her from the dancers to the bar where Richard was still dispensing drinks.

'Hello, love,' said Richard cheerfully, 'want some more wine? How about you, Ramsay?'

James accepted a whisky and soda, but Eleanor shook her head, content to stand and just listen as the two men talked about the prospects of the England cricket team on their Australian tour.

Suddenly she became aware that James was talking to her.

'I think I'd better be on my way, Eleanor. I'm lunching with Mother and Dad tomorrow, and I promised to spend the morning reporting on my London trip, so

I need some sleep to prepare me for a session with the old man.'

Richard went off to find Harriet while Eleanor looked up at James dreamily.

'Thank you for coming.'

'The thanks are all on my side. Only one drawback, though, I can't take you home.' He grinned down at her. 'That's usually the best part of the evening.'

'Possibly.' Eleanor's tone was dry. 'I think I'll call it a day, too. My niece will have me awake at daybreak, no doubt, and this lot look set for a couple of hours yet. I rarely stay the course at these things.'

Harriet returned with Richard, hand outstretched.

'We were very pleased you could come, James.' Her smile was warm. 'Come again. You're welcome any time.'

'Thank you both very much for having me,' he said, kissing the proffered hand, to Harriet's delight. 'Actually, if you don't mind I'd like to come and collect Eleanor tomorrow afternoon, and take her home.'

Eleanor looked at him in surprise.

'Honestly, James, there's no need.'

'I'd like to,' he said firmly.

Harriet beamed.

'Of course, James, have some tea with us before you start back. We haven't really had much of a chance to talk to you tonight. Look, I must get back to being a hostess. Richard, I think some glasses need refilling. See you tomorrow, then, I must mingle now.'

Left alone in the hall, James said:

'Walk me to the car, Eleanor.' The blue eyes were persuasive. 'Just for a moment. The car's parked along the lane.'

They left unnoticed. Outside there was a new moon, and the night was very still and cold. Eleanor shivered as the cold air struck chill through the thin silk of her dress. James took off his jacket and wrapped it around her, warm from his body heat, giving her the feeling she was still in his arms. As they strolled down the garden the beauty of the night filled her with a feeling of elation. Compounded partly of alcohol, I suspect, she thought.

'Do you mind my coming for you tomorrow?' he asked.

'No, I'd like it very much. It was kind of you to suggest it.'

They had reached the Porsche, which gleamed darkly in the dim light from the street lamp. James leaned against the bonnet.

'Don't credit me with too much virtue—I'm just getting my own way.'

'You'll be cold without your jacket,' murmured Eleanor, changing the subject.

'Keep me warm, then.'

He slid his arms round her under the jacket, holding her as close as though they were still dancing. He leaned back against the car, holding her off balance so that she lay against him unresisting, her breathing quickening as his head bent to hers and he began to kiss her with small, swift kisses that began gently, then lengthened and deepened until her body was no longer lax in his arms, but urgent against his as his hands strayed up her spine and back, moulding her against him. Her lips opened to the insistence of his, and her own responded to his insistent caress until she became mindless with pleasure.

James tore his mouth away and held her so tightly against him it was difficult to tell which heart hammered more loudly.

'Sit in the car with me for a moment.' His whisper was urgent.

'No,' she whispered back.

'Why not?'

'There must be a dozen good reasons, even if I can't think of one right at this moment. In fact, I can't think clearly at all.' She gave a shaky little laugh. 'James—I detested you so much last week it doesn't seem logical suddenly to be feeling like this.'

'To hell with logic.' His voice was rough and uneven, but he straightened and stood her squarely on her feet. He put one finger under her chin and raised her face to his.

'At the present rate of improvement think how you'll feel by next week!' His tone was deliberately light and mocking. 'Go in now before you freeze. Keep the jacket, I'll collect it tomorrow. Go straight to bed.' He unlocked the car and got in, unwinding the window to lean out. 'Don't get waylaid by any amorous medicos on your way in.'

'I'll think about it. Goodnight.'

He gave her a salute, then let in the clutch and drove off. Eleanor went quickly back into the house, found Harriet and said goodnight, then went to bed and instantly to sleep.

# CHAPTER FIVE

ELEANOR woke to find bright sunlight streaming across her bed and Edward standing at the foot of it, holding a steaming mug with extreme care. He looked at her anxiously.

'Mummy said I wasn't to wake you, but if you were awake I was to give you this.'

Eleanor struggled sleepily to sit up and took the coffee beaker gratefully.

'That's lovely, Edward, and I suppose you did wake me up, but if it's breakfast time it's just as well.'

Edward's face creased in a cheeky grin.

'You're a bit behind, Auntie El—this is elevenses, not breakfast. See you!'

Eleanor shot out of bed and gasped as she saw the time. After eleven, and she had slept like the dead, oblivious of departing party guests and early rising children alike. Rushing through a swift shower and getting herself dressed took only a few minutes. She was in the habit of keeping a few spare things at Harriet's, and quickly scrambled into a pair of ancient washed-out blue jeans and an elderly blue and green striped rugby shirt she found at the bottom of a drawer. She pulled on a pair of battered plimsolls and hastily braided her hair, securing the end with an elastic band.

Harriet was beating up Yorkshire pudding batter at the kitchen table when Eleanor went in looking the picture of guilt.

'Harriet, I am sorry! I never sleep late—I just don't know what hit me, utter oblivion for about ten hours.'

78

'Not to worry, love, you obviously needed it. Would you like something to eat?'

'It's a bit near to lunchtime, thanks. Where is everybody?'

'Richard's taken the boys off into Tollmarston Woods for a few minutes and Victoria's in the playpen in the conservatory. More coffee?'

'Yes, please. What time did everyone leave last night?'

'Oh, two-ish, I think. It seems to have been reasonably successful.' Harriet shot an impish look at Eleanor. 'I assume I may take it that you enjoyed yourself? Come on, give. Did James come up to expectations? He never let you out of his clutches once he arrived, Eleanor, obviously he had no intention of circulating.'

Eleanor leaned her elbows on the table and gazed out of the kitchen window.

'It was a fantastic evening, Harriet. I told him all about Nick while we had supper—you didn't mind our sneaking off to Richard's study?'

'No, silly, of course not.'

Eleanor said casually:

'What did you think of him?'

Harriet pushed the bowl to one side and sat down, coffee mug in both hands.

'In a word, little sister, wow! Poor Althea nearly expired with frustration. She arrived more or less at the same time as James, so I couldn't avoid introducing him. He's very clever. After the briefest of polite interchanges he somehow implied that, desolate as he was at the prospect, he had to tear himself away for some pressing reason. When the pressing reason turned out to be detaching you from young Chris Tate in record time her eyes nearly popped out. Seriously, though, he's very premier league, Eleanor. Are you sure you can cope?'

'Cope with what? And before you expound on the theme, yes, I think I can cope very well, thank you.' Eleanor stood up and stretched. 'Apart from anything else, I've had the best night's sleep in years, which has given me a great enthusiasm for potato peeling, so pass me a knife.'

'I won't turn down a good offer. Ah, that's Vicky starting to protest, so I'll deal with her if you're going to be noble. The house is reasonably tidy, I had a quick attack on it earlier on.'

Eleanor set about the potatoes with despatch, and had prepared brussels sprouts and cauliflower by the time Harriet returned with a refurbished Victoria, who immediately held out her arms to Eleanor.

Eleanor sat with the baby on her lap while Harriet went on with the lunch. The glorious smell of roasting beef had brought the dogs in, and they gave Harriet no peace until she fed them. She examined Eleanor more carefully as she stood up.

'Where on earth did you dig that shirt up, Eleanor? I thought it had been put out for the church jumble sale.'

'It was in a drawer in my room. I only brought that thick yellow sweater, and I thought this would be more the thing for whatever game the boys want to play after lunch.'

'You don't have to play with them, El, it isn't as though you have to earn your bed and board, or something.'

'I enjoy playing with them.' Eleanor was indignant. 'Anyway, James won't be here until tea-time, I can be a bit more respectable by then.' She wandered over to the window, Vicky comfortably balanced on one hip.

'Break out the squash and the sherry. The gentlemen of the household have returned.'

'Gentlemen!' wailed Harriet, as three mud-en-crusted, glowing boys erupted into the kitchen, followed at a more indolent pace by their father. 'Wellies outside, you lot, then wash and change before you do anything.'

'It was super,' said Charles breathlessly, 'we rolled down this hill . . .'

'And there was gooey mud at the bottom,' interrupted David rapturously, 'and I rolled over and over in it.'

'So I see,' said his mother grimly. 'Where was Daddy during this period of unconfined joy?'

'Oh, he was watching birds through his binoculars,' said Edward, grinning, 'he sort of lost sight of us for a minute.'

His father gave him a playful cuff and sent him off with the others, then slid an arm placatingly round his wife's slender waist.

'Sorry, darling, but the birds were the feathered kind, I assure you. I didn't notice the mudbath.'

'You,' said Harriet balefully, 'were supposed to keep them reasonably clean!' But her protests died as he kissed her.

'Shall I take Victoria somewhere else?' asked Eleanor innocently, 'or will you just pretend I'm not here and carry on regardless?'

'Enough of your cheek, Eleanor.' Richard released his wife reluctantly and went off to get the sherry. 'Both you girls having one?'

Harriet looked at the clock.

'We may even manage two if you hurry.'

As Richard handed Eleanor her glass he noticed her outfit.

'Isn't that my old rugby shirt?' he said, astonished. 'It looks a bit different on you, thought it had gone years ago. Mind, I don't want to appear rude, but isn't Ramsay coming to collect you this afternoon? Hardly the rig for a tryst, El.'

'Yes, he is, and no, it isn't a tryst—that's a good word, Richard—it's just a lift home. I promise I'll change before then, and even if I don't it won't matter.'

'Take no notice, love,' said Harriet comfortably, 'have another sherry while the vegetables are doing.'

'Not for me. I had rather more to drink than usual last night; I expect that's why I slept so heavily.'

'Better than Mogadon,' said Richard. 'Perhaps I could prescribe white wine to my insomniac patients as a substitute. Actually, though, Eleanor, I think you've been overdoing it quite considerably lately, so nature took over and knocked you out. The result is splendid anyway, you look positively blooming this morning.'

'Some wine!' Harriet was sceptical. 'Come on, let's get this lunch on the road. You carve, Richard, will you do the gravy, El, and I'll see to the rest. We'll eat out here today for speed.'

Soon everyone was consuming large quantities of beef and vegetables, followed by left-overs from the party desserts. Harriet refused Eleanor's offer to wash up afterwards.

'No, darling, if you really must play with the boys do it now. You'll probably have indigestion, but I'd rather you were somewhat more respectable as soon as possible. That shirt is a trifle tight!'

Eleanor laughed, put Vicky in the pushchair and wheeled her out into the garden to watch her aunt's initiation into the mysteries of rugby football. Edward was just learning the game at his new school, and very proudly issued a stream of instructions on line-outs, reverse passes, with incessant shouts of 'off-side' and much blowing of his whistle. The game finally deteriorated into a wholesale scrummage which ended with all four breathless participants in a hopeless tangle on the lawn.

'Help me up, boys,' gasped Eleanor, 'I'm done in. I'll have to get in some strict training before I can hope to make the team!'

To her embarrassment the helping hands that grasped hers were larger and harder than any of those belonging to her nephews. James whisked her to her feet and stood there smiling, the boys immediately quiet and shy. Eleanor felt much the same as she met the blue glint in the eyes that swept her from head to foot with appreciation.

'You'll never make a forward, Eleanor.' The deep voice was full of laughter. 'Perhaps you could try out on the wing.'

'Hello, James, you're early; I'll get it in the neck from Harriet.' Eleanor laughed ruefully, making vain attempts to smooth her hair. 'I was supposed to be all changed and tidy by the time you came. Shake hands with Mr Ramsay, boys. James, these are Edward, Charles and David, in order of seniority.'

James shook hands with each one formally.

'Perhaps you'd care to have me for a substitute while your aunt changes,' he offered. 'I was considered a fairly useful wing-threequarter in school. Maybe I could give you a few pointers.'

His offer was enthusiastically received by the boys, but Eleanor looked doubtfully at his clothes. Last night's offwhite cord jeans had been joined by a black V-necked sweater over a white shirt.

'Won't you get dirty?' she queried.

'Possibly Not to worry, everything's washable. Off you go while we get down to things of male importance.' He gave her a slap on her rear, grinning impenitently at her affronted look, then became quickly involved in the intricacies of correct scrummaging.

Eleanor flew into the house, to meet Harriet emerging from the kitchen.

'James has arrived, I'd better change.'

'He saw you like that?' Harriet groaned. 'Where have you put him?'

'I haven't put him anywhere. He's rolling round on the lawn teaching the boys how to play rugby! Harriet, can I borrow a scarf?'

'Anything you like—in my dressing table drawer. I'd better find Richard quickly and get him to call those monsters off.'

Eleanor raced upstairs, found the black silk scarf she wanted, and went back to her own room to replace the disreputable jeans and shirt with her black cords and yellow sweater and set to work on her hair. She unravelled the thick braid at top speed, brushed it vigorously, then secured the heavy mass at the nape of her neck with the black scarf, letting the ends mingle with her hair. A flick of mascara and lip-gloss, a spray of perfume, then she was running down the stairs to find the sportsmen were now all indoors, everyone settled in the living-room, the two men holding tankards of beer and the boys listening, with varying degrees of interest, to the various merits of English and Welsh style of play. Harriet sat with Vicky on her lap trying to make sense of the discussion.

James detached himself from the group as Eleanor came into the room, and sat beside her on a settee. The boys soon drifted out to play again as the talk grew more adult and uninteresting, and the four remaining chatted amicably while the baby dozed on Harriet's shoulder until she eventually woke up and was handed to her father while Eleanor and Harriet went out to fetch in the tea-trolley.

Replete with beef sandwiches, rich fruit cake and gentlemen's relish on toast, James and Eleanor made their farewells and were soon in the Porsche, speeding back through the dark countryside.

James drove in silence for a while, then said:

'The atmosphere of felicity your sister's family generates is impressive; enough to convert the most hardened of cynics.'

'They have a very good life,' agreed Eleanor. 'I think because both of them are completely fulfilled in their vocations. I'm sure you're aware that Harriet considers the job of wife and mother just as important to her as practising medicine is to Richard.'

'It's plain that she enjoys what she does to the full, but, at very short acquaintance, there's something else that comes through very strongly; the basic ingredient of their marriage, I imagine.'

'Oh?' Eleanor looked at his dimly-lit profile with interest.

'Richard is obviously very much in love with his wife, despite several years of marriage and four children, and, I think, she with him. It's this that radiates the atmosphere of warmth.'

Eleanor was pensive, absently watching the long, sure hands on the wheel.

'I suppose you're right. I expect I take it for granted because they've always been like that, since the first day they met. I'm not naïve enough to believe that all marriages are the same.'

'Far from it. I fondly believed that I might achieve

something like it once. No doubt you've heard.'
James's voice was wry.

'I was told you were engaged, but the lady married
someone else.'

'Your informant omitted the fact that Erica blithely
told me it was all off exactly one week before the ceremony. She'd brought off a much better matrimonial
catch.'

'No,' Eleanor kept her eyes on the approaching lights
of the town, 'I hadn't realised. It must have been a
shattering experience.'

James laughed, unconcerned.

'Actually, looking back on it, I now realise I had a
fortunate escape. I was much younger then. I hope
I've matured in the interim, but the last time I en-
countered Erica at some function she was exactly the
same, blonde curls, gurgling laugh complete.'

Eleanor was quiet, trying to visualise a younger,
softer James, desolate in the loss of his blonde lady-
love. Involuntarily she smiled at the incongruous vapid
doll she conjured up, and James glanced sideways, his
eyebrows raised.

'What's tickling you, Eleanor?'

'The thought of you completely subjugated by any
woman, however fascinating. I get the impression you
don't think too highly of my sex in general.'

'There are enormous compensations,' he said, as
they turned into Mill Crescent. 'The female of the
species has a great deal to offer in many ways. It's the
thought of being tied to one permanently that is
inclined to chill the soul.'

'Tactless, but honest,' said Eleanor lightly, gathering
her belongings as he brought the car into the kerb.

James caught her arm.

'Don't dash off, Eleanor. I was hoping you'd come

and have a meal with me. There are quite a few things about the Brazilian contract I'd like to discuss.'

Eleanor looked at him levelly.

'On a Sunday evening, James? Won't it wait until the morning?'

'No,' he said flatly.

'Well, frankly, after Harriet's roast beef lunch, plus all that food we consumed at teatime, I don't think I need much more to eat today. Perhaps we could compromise.'

'What do you suggest?'

Eleanor hestitated a second, then threw caution to the winds.

'You could come up to the flat if you like—I'll find something to drink, and later on I could manage an omelette and some salad. Does the idea appeal?'

'Strongly!' James's eyes were gleaming as he bent towards her. 'Does your landlady approve of male visitors?'

'I have no idea,' said Eleanor softly. 'The subject has never previously arisen.'

He lifted her hand and kissed it in apology.

'Forgive me. I forget you play to a different set of rules—will you be patient with me?'

'I've managed it for the past three weeks. I see no reason to change now.' Her voice was tart as she opened the car door and got out. James followed with her suitcase and a cardboard box. As they reached the front door she realised the house was in darkness.

'Mrs Jenkins is probably in church.' Eleanor handed him her key.

Upstairs in the flat James looked around in approval at the uncluttered living-room. Eleanor had covered the chairs and sofa in coarse brown linen to contrast with Mrs Jenkins's dull gold carpet, and she had made thick cotton curtains, white, with a print of large yellow sunflowers. One wall held shelves filled with books and records, with a modest record-player at one end.

'So this is your retreat,' he said, prowling round reading book-titles. 'Did you furnish it yourself?'

'Not originally, but now Mrs J. and I have an amicable understanding. She sees to the paint and provides the carpets and furniture, and I can do what I like about curtains, covers, odds and ends. Then in the summer I help her in the garden in the evenings, and if there's enough sun I sit out there after work sometimes.'

'You like the sun?'

'Mm, love it, and happily I tan very easily. James, make yourself at home, I must run down and see if Mrs Jenkins has any milk.'

Eleanor went quickily downstairs, where everything was in darkness. She switched on the lights and went through to the kitchen, where she took a pint of milk from the fridge. As she shut it she noticed a note taped to the door.

'Gone to my sister's until Monday, Eleanor, help yourself to anything you need.'

Eleanor ran back upstairs to find James browsing through record sleeves. He turned and smiled, his height and sheer masculinity dominating the confines of her small sitting-room.

'All in perfect alphabetical order, like the perfect little paragon you are. May I play something?'

'Help yourself.' Eleanor went into the kitchen with the milk and the coardboard box thrust on her by Harriet as they said goodbye. It contained a selection of delicacies, including a plastic container of ready-mixed salad, a crusty brown loaf, some Stilton and a bottle of white wine.

Eleanor smiled as she saw the latter; Richard obviously intended her to go on sleeping soundly!

'James,' she called, 'I have whisky, which you can have with ginger ale, if you like. There's brandy, too, but I thought you'd probably prefer that with coffee later. Richard insists on providing me with it for medicinal purposes.'

The voice of Barbra Streisand came from the other room as he joined her in the kitchen.

'Whisky and water, please—fairly long. What are you having?'

'Richard has kindly donated a bottle of white wine, the one I was drinking last night, so I'll have a glass now as well as with our meal. Will you open it, please?'

They went back to the sitting-room with the drinks and Eleanor switched on the gas-fire set in the fireplace. She curled up on the rug in front of it, her back against one of the chairs, and waved James to the sofa.

'What was this urgent matter you wanted to discuss, James?'

He stretched out relaxed, long legs stretched out before him, and looked down at her.

'I'm going to Brazil in two weeks' time. The hotel construction job I'm hoping to pull off is for a company that's part French, part Brazilian. They have one hotel in Copacabana already, and want to build another in Lagoa Azul, a bit further along the coast. I need to be there for a few days for talks with Jean-Paul Gérard, the French top man, also with José Carvalho and Helio Souza Lima on the Brazilian side. I would like you to come with me. My father assures me your Portuguese is fluent—naturally!—and old José Carvalho would appreciate that, his English is a bit eccentric. It's obviously important to have all the nuances of the deal perfectly clear. This is where, I hope you come in. You can sit in and record all the discussions, also give me a hand on the entertaining side.'

James leaned forward as Eleanor said nothing, looking up at him wide-eyed.

'Well, Eleanor, what do you say?'

'Heavens, James, you don't need to ask twice! I've been as far as Portugal and had no difficulty with the language there, but in my wildest dreams I never imagined getting as far as Brazil.' She jumped up, suddenly unable to keep still. 'When will we go?'

He rose with her, smiling down into her animated face.

'Tuesday week. I imagine you have a current passport?'

She nodded blissfully.

'Good. We should be away about four or five days, depending on how things go. I already know Jean-Paul Gérard, he and his wife Christiane have an apartment in Ipanema.'

Eleanor sighed rapturously.

'Is there really such a place? I thought it was just a song. Will it be hot at this time of year? What clothes shall I take?'

'November's just starting to get really hot, by our standards. You'll need cotton dresses by day, something gorgeous like that dress last night for the evenings, and your bikini, of course. We'll stay at the Ouro Prato hotel in Copacabana. That's French-owned, actually, connections of Jean-Paul's. You can walk straight out of the hotel in swimming gear, just across the Avenida Atlantica and there's the beach.'

Eleanor's eyes were glowing with anticipation as she suddenly remembered her role as hostess.

'Come into the kitchen with me, James. You can

talk to me while I find us something to eat.'

James followed her obediently and poured her another glass of wine.

'Can I help?'

'No, thanks. The space is a bit limited for someone your dimensions. Just entertain me while I do my haute-cuisine bit. Do you like prawns?'

'Yes, ma'am. By the way, what did your landlady say about a male dining with you?'

'Nothing.' Eleanor concentrated on opening a tin of prawns and kept her eyes down. 'She's away at her sister's for the weekend, there was a note on the fridge.'

There was a small silence, and she looked up to see him watching her, a little smile lifting the corners of his mouth.

'Would you have invited me in if you'd known?' James balanced back in one of the kitchen chairs.

Eleanor thought for a moment.

'Very probably not. But as you *are* here you might as well stay; particularly since you've thrown out the lure of a trip to Brazil . . .' She stopped short, flushing scarlet.

James threw back his head and roared.

'Sweetheart, I don't think the offer of a few days' working holiday, even in Brazil, is going to gain me access to your bed, is it?'

'Not if I'm in it too, no,' said Eleanor acidly, going on swiftly with her preparations. The prawns were soon simmering in butter with tomatoes and onions while she sliced brown bread and transferred the salad to a bowl. She handed James cutlery and plates.

'You can set the table while I'm beating the eggs. You don't mind eating out here?'

'Not in the least. I was just thinking what a cosy, domesticated little scene this is, just like Darby and Joan.'

She pushed a strand of hair back from her forehead and gave him a grin as she filled the coffee-percolator.

'Careful, best to avoid thoughts like that. The prospect of your chilled soul—I quote—might give you indigestion!'

James watched her with evident pleasure as she poured the egg mixture into the sizzling butter in a small omelette pan and carefully chivvied it round, her tongue between her teeth in concentration. She slid one omelette on to a waiting hot plate, added more butter to the pan and poured in the remaining eggs. Seconds later another omelette was ready and the prawn mixture distributed between the two. Silence fell as they both fell to with enthusiasm.

'You are a distinctly versatile lady,' said James, his mouth inelegantly full. 'The perfect secretary, cook par excellence, adored aunt and highly decorative to boot. There must be some area which defeats you?'

Eleanor buttered a slice of bread thoughtfully, frowning slightly.

'I have difficulty in making new friends, I suppose; no talent for casual relationships.'

The overtone of intimacy in James's smile made her uneasy.

'I'm not asking a casual relationship of you, Eleanor.'

'Of course.' Eleanor was brisk as she jumped up to remove his plate. 'You're my employer, which is quite different. Will you have some of this Stilton?'

'Yes, thank you. No biscuits, though, I'll have more of this bread. That was a truly superb omelette—my compliments.'

Eleanor bobbed a curtsy as she brought the cheese-board.

'Shall I pour our coffee now, or when we've finished eating?'

'After I wash up. No, I insist, let's drink it in the other room with some of that brandy you promised.'

James overrode all her protests, and in a very short time the kitchen was immaculate and they were both settled on the couch, drinking coffee and brandy, and thrashing out the details of the Brazilian trip.

'Who will cope with my routine work while I'm away?' she asked.

'Frances Marshall, with the aid of a temp if necessary. Anything she feels must be left to you can be left until we get back. We'll be away less than a week.'

James rose and poured another small brandy for her, a larger one for himself, then sat closer and put his arm round her as they sat drinking it.

Eleanor sat stiffly erect at first, to James's obvious amusement, but gradually she relaxed and eventually he put their glasses on the table and settled back, pulling her firmly against him.

'That's a good girl.' The deep, caressing note in his voice had a very unsettling effect.

'I intend to be just that.' Her voice was muffled.

James laughed, his arm tightening.

'Darling girl, I don't know what stories you've had fed to you about me, but you shy away as though rape and seduction were my normal routine!'

Eleanor giggled involuntarily.

'You could hardly call rape routine!' She turned her face up to his to meet eyes that had darkened slightly and were intent on hers.

'It might possibly be seduction, Eleanor,' he said very softly, 'but it wouldn't be rape, would it? Come on, little paragon, face the truth, there's been an unmistakable current between us since the first moment I laid eyes on you. Are you going to deny it?'

She shook her head slowly, her eyes still held by his, then her lids drooped as his head bent and his mouth settled lightly but surely on hers. She was only half aware of the hand that released her hair at the nape of her neck, freeing it to tumble in a dark shining cascade over her shoulders as his fingers played through it and his mouth became more possessive. She made no protest as he lifted her across his knees and wholly into his arms. Her small sound of dissent was unable to deter the long hand that insinuated itself so smoothly beneath her sweater and stroked her heated skin with such expertise. The pressure of his mouth increased until her lips opened naturally to his insistence and her heartbeats accelerated, keeping rhythm with his as his hands sought and found her breasts, making her gasp in a mixture of delight and fear.

In the turmoil of panic and pleasure that his hands and lips were inducing Eleanor hardly noticed that she was sliding lower and lower until she realised with a jolt that his long body was practically prone on hers. She tore her mouth away from his and frantically struggled upright, pushing James away and trying to hide her flaming cheeks behind the chaotic fall of hair.

James yanked her sweater down and wrapped his arms tightly round her, holding her hard against him.

'I'm sorry, sorry,' he whispered. 'Don't tremble, for God's sake! You make me feel like Jack the Ripper. Is my touch such an offence, Eleanor? If you find me utterly repulsive just say so.'

'That's not the problem at all.' Eleanor's voice was huskily fierce as she pulled away from him a little, vainly trying to push back her hair. 'Quite the reverse, in fact. James, I'm terrified.'

'Good God—of me?'

'No, no,' she said desperately, 'of me! I'm apprehensive of all that cataclysm of—of sensation. It's so physical and unmanageable. James, please don't think me unreasonable, but would you mind very much if I asked you to go home now? Don't get all cold and distant, it's merely that I have to accustom myself to this sort of thing by degrees, I think. You must think me all kinds of an idiot.'

He stood up, pulling her up with him and holding her close.

'It's an incomparable feeling, Eleanor, you can't fight it for ever. There's a lot going on outside that ivory tower of yours, you know; I think it's time you rejoined the rest of us in the outside world.'

'You're as bad as Richard!' Eleanor's expression was rueful as she pushed him gently away. 'Apparently he says I have a *'princesse lointaine'* look on occasion. Doesn't come over as a fanciful type, does he?'

'Accurate, though. I know what he means.' James smiled down at her. 'Bedtime, now I think, princess. All on your own too, before you start making suspicious noises. See you in the morning.'

Eleanor went out with him on to the landing.

'Thank you for the meal,' he said. 'I'll see the door is locked downstairs. Eleanor?'

'Yes, James?'

'Just one goodnight kiss.'

She lifted her face obediently.

'No, Eleanor, I want *you* to kiss *me*.'

The look in his eyes did something strange to her knees, and without hesitation she stood on tiptoe, put her arms around his neck and kissed him tentatively. He stood passively for a moment, receiving the shy pressure of her lips, then he locked his arms round her

and kissed her with an intensity that left her breathless
long after she heard the front door close and the sound
of the car starting up.

She drifted back into the kitchen in a trance-like
state, going through the motions of making tea like an
automaton. She carried her mug into the sitting room
and subsided on to the settee, staring absently into the
flickering artificial flames of the gas fire. Gradually her
euphoric glow diminished; tendrils of doubt curled in
her mind like rising mist and she drank the hot tea
convulsively in an effort to regain her usual calm.

Whatever that is, she thought sceptically. I'm beginning to wonder if I'll ever be entirely the same
person again. Rising abruptly, impatient with herself,
she decided to have a bath. The warm water lapping
against her skin had the desired soothing effect and
eventually she towelled herself dry and sat in front of
her dressing-table mirror to brush her heavy length of
hair.

The girl who looked back at her was almost a
stranger. Her habitual mask of reserve, acquired with
such painstaking care, had completely disappeared, and
its absence revealed a vital, glowing face whose brilliant
dark eyes held an expression quite unfamiliar to their
owner. I feel like a butterfly newly burst from its chry-
salis, she thought, staring at her reflection, or do I
mean a snail without its shell? Either way the overwhelming sensation was utter vulnerability, and
Eleanor's misgivings returned in full force.

In her first delighted reaction to James's invitation
to Rio she had blithely disregarded what exactly he
might expect of her. Perhaps he imagined she had
agreed to a great deal more than her normal secretarial
function. Perhaps he was used to a secretary who was
willing to undertake extramural activities she herself

would most definitely refuse. Perhaps ... Perhaps you'd better wait until you're asked, you suspicious idiot, she said out loud in exasperation, and pulled her nightdress over her head with an impatient yank. For heaven's sake, all the man wants is an efficient secretary, who happens to have the slightly unusual advantage of speaking Portuguese, so stop behaving like the heroine in a Victorian melodrama. You're not likely to have a chance like this again, ever.

Feeling better after her essay in self-discipline, she turned off the fire and the lights and settled herself in bed, but her body refused to relax and her mind obstinately seethed with doubts and speculation. The silence was suddenly shattered abruptly by the ring of the telephone alongside the bed, and she jerked bolt upright, switching on the bedside lamp as she lifted the receiver warily.

'It's only me,' came James's voice in swift reassurance.

'Thank the Lord for that,' said Eleanor tartly. 'You startled me—it's gone eleven.'

'I know, but I had this nagging feeling you were having doubts about the Rio trip.'

Eleanor looked at the receiver with surprise, feeling as Aladdin must have done when the genie appeared from the lamp.

'Yes, I was, actually. How did you know, James?'

'Oh, I knew! For starters, I think I should have made it crystal clear that there are positively no strings.'

There was a short, pregnant silence.

'I—I'm not sure what you mean,' said Eleanor primly.

'Yes, you are.' James sounded amused but decisive. 'I'll lay it on the line. All I expect is your usual secretarial expertise, plus help with any language diffi-

culties, also the not inconsiderable pleasure of your
company in the evenings. Apart from that nothing, or
'*nada*' as they say in Brazil. Is that precise enough for
you, or would you like it in writing?'

Eleanor smiled dreamily up at the ceiling and
stretched luxuriously under the bedclothes.

'Your word will do very nicely, James, thank you.
I'll be honest, though, and admit to a severe attack of
cold feet.'

'I thought so. Now you can sleep in peace.' James's
voice dropped to a caressing note. 'For some reason I
forgot to say goodnight when I left, princess. Sweet
dreams.'

'Goodnight, James, thank you for bringing me
home.'

'I hope I'm not completely accurate when I say the
pleasure was all mine, Eleanor. *Ciao*.'

Eleanor put the phone down and stared pleasurably
into the darkness, mind and body now completely
relaxed as she drifted off to sleep on what felt remarkably like a pink cloud.

# CHAPTER SIX

TEN days later Eleanor sat tense with anticipation in the seat of a Transatlantic jet, James deeply asleep beside her. She smiled inwardly as she looked at his profile, assertive even in repose. It would have been hardly surprising if she were in the same condition, but she was far too excited to sleep now that Rio de Janeiro was only a short period of flying time away.

The past few days had been a kaleidoscope of hard work, frantic shopping, and an immense effort to leave everything as highly organised as possible for Frances. Eleanor lay relaxed, thinking with amusement of Harriet's face when she learned of the Rio trip. Her shriek of excitement had brought Richard at the double, and they had both bombarded Eleanor with questions. Then had come a weekend of frenzied shopping with Harriet, a dinner with James, at a restaurant this time, then a period of intensive clearing up at the office while James went on a trip to the London office before leaving. It was hard to believe that they were now high above the Atlantic, and shortly the beautiful bay of Guanabara would appear below them before they touched down at Galeao airport.

James had warned her against disappointment, as the view was often obscured by morning mist because, contrary to Eleanor's preconceived ideas, Rio was not always bathed in sunshine, but often wet, and nearly always humid.

He stirred alongside her, stretching and yawning.

'Couldn't you even doze, Eleanor?' he asked sleepily. 'You'll be suffering from jet lag when we land.'

'I couldn't.' Her smile was apologetic. 'I feel too keyed up; a bit immature of me, I suppose.'

'Refreshing, rather. Here comes the stewardess, would you like coffee or a drink?'

'Coffee, please, I'm intoxicated enough already with excitement!'

After the coffee Eleanor went off to freshen herself up for their arrival. Her face glowed with anticipation as she touched up her make-up in the washroom mirror, then smoothed her hair more firmly into its knot and sprayed a little perfume on throat and wrists before rejoining James.

As she sat down the warning lights flashed on and they fastened their seat-belts. Eleanor's stomach muscles tightened, but she smiled brilliantly at James, then turned to peer through the window as the plane began its circling descent.

'James, my luck is in—there's no mist, just burning blue sky, and down there the water is glittering in the sunlight.'

He held her hand, enjoying the swift expressions of pleasure and anticipation chasing across her face.

'Can you see the Corcovado yet?' he asked indulgently.

'What's that? Oh, look at all those little islands in the bay, like a scattering of jewels over the sea—James, is that mountain with the statue the Corcovado?'

James leaned closer and followed her pointing hand.

The high peak of the Corcovado glittered in the morning sun, topped with its great statue of Christ the Redemptor, arms outstretched in eternal blessing over the city.

Eleanor twisted round in her seat to look at James,

her face white and her dark eyes incandescent.

'It's unbelievably beautiful! How can I ever thank you enough for bringing me?'

'Something will come to mind, no doubt. Now what?' as she gasped, her eyes widening as she watched the blue water rushing up to meet them.

'James—it looks as though we're touching down on the sea!'

'Not quite. Both airports, internal and international, are right on the water's edge. There, you see, you can open your eyes now, the wheels have just made contact with terra firma.'

The glamorous stewardess smiled very warmly indeed at James as they took leave of her and made their way into the airport terminal. The heat struck Eleanor like a blow, and her ivory crocheted cotton dress and jacket felt like chainmail suddenly. She eyed James's lightweight suit in sympathy; he must be even warmer than she was.

'This heat is quite something, James, and what's that smell?' She sniffed appreciatively as they hurried along. 'It seems like a combination of perfume and cigar smoke . . .'

'With a slight overtone of garlic,' James added, 'only it's not cigars, that's how the cigarettes smell here. Incidentally, most of the men here use perfume as well as the women, hence the atmosphere.'

With surprisingly little delay they were through Customs and making for the exit, a porter following with the luggage. Eleanor looked around her eagerly, trying to take in every detail of the crowd, which was colourful in the extreme. There were elegant, well-groomed, wealthy ladies in brilliant colours and poorer, somewhat shapeless women in black, a plethora of men in white suits, obvious tourists in gaudy clothes, instantly recognisable by the amount of cameras strung about them. There were the inevitable nuns, and in contrast, young girls who, without exception, were the most gorgeous Eleanor had ever seen in such quantity.

'James, do look at all these delectable creatures, they all look like Miss World!'

'Only at this age, unfortunately; they tend to put on weight once they marry and start to produce large numbers of babies,' he said drily, then broke off. 'At last—there's Jean-Paul, late as usual.'

A slim dark man was pushing his way through the crowd, his tanned face split in a wide white grin. He embraced James, but his black eyes were riveted on Eleanor with an expression of exaggerated awe.

'James, *bienvenu*.' His voice was husky and loaded with charm. 'You are obviously well, and this lady you would have me believe is your secretary? What stroke of good fortune enabled you to find her?'

'She was a legacy,' said James, without expression. 'Eleanor, may I present Jean-Paul Gérard. Jean-Paul, this is Eleanor Hunt.'

'*Enchanté, mademoiselle.*' The elegant Frenchman raised her hand to his lips, black eyes gleaming with appreciation.

'How do you do, Monsieur Gérard.' Eleanor was composed, though a little pink-cheeked as she smiled at him.

'Actually,' drawled James, looking sideways at her deliberately, 'just a minor detail, old boy, but it's *Mrs* Hunt.'

Jean-Paul shrugged expressively.

'How could it be otherwise—unless Englishmen are all blind!'

He took hold of Eleanor's elbow as he shepherded her with care through the crowded terminal towards the exit, closely followed by James and a porter with the luggage.

Eleanor felt obliged to put matters straight.

'I'm a widow, Monsieur Gérard.'

Immediately he stopped dead, causing a considerable hold-up as he gazed down at her in disbelief.

'That one so young should be a widow! *Pauvre petite!*'

James sounded irritable as they got under way again.

'Could you postpone the Gallic charm bit until we reach the car, Jean-Paul? I for one could do with a shower, a drink and lunch, and I'm sure Eleanor could too.'

Jean-Paul ushered them apologetically into the white Citroën waiting illegally just outside, saw to the stowing away of the luggage, tipped the porter, and they were soon speeding their way through the beautiful city.

Eleanor sat beside Jean-Paul in the front of the car, twisting this way and that in an effort to take in every aspect of the fascinating panorama of Rio. The pavements, inlaid with black and white mosaic, were punctuated at intervals with the bright umbrellas over the outside tables of the numerous cafés and bars, and the buildings were a mixture of old Portuguese Colonial sandwiched between towering modern skyscrapers. Over everything the golden yellow sunlight poured its warmth, shining down on the noonday throng of people, their skins every variation of colour from white to black. Soon they left the city and headed towards Copacabana, the road here and there slicing suddenly through the mountainside via short brilliantly lit tunnels. As they passed Leblon James pointed out the Sugar Loaf Mountain, cable cars strung from its conical peak to give the intrepid traveller unrivalled views of the city below.

Eleanor was ecstatic, all attempt at composure quite abandoned.

'It's fabulous,' she said blissfully, smiling over her shoulder at James. 'I know that's an overworked word, but really, how else can one describe all this?'

They eventually reached the great white and gold curve of Copacabana, with its luxury hotels sweeping in a great semi-circle at the edge of a narrow strip of sand constantly battered by the towering white surf of the Atlantic, where the Ouro Prato proved to be one of the older buildings. Eleanor was enchanted with its gleaming white façade, broken here and there by decorative balconies, many with exotic plants trailing from them. Its terrace was filled with people lunching with all the serious attention the Brazilians devote to their food.

Jean-Paul ushered Eleanor and James through the foyer to the reception desk, and introduced them to the manager, who summoned a boy to take up the luggage and show them to their rooms.

'I will reserve a table on the terrace while you inspect your rooms,' said Jean-Paul, 'then perhaps you will join me when you come down.'

'Fine,' agreed James, taking Eleanor by the arm. 'We'll be down in ten minutes.'

The porter led the way to the lift, where they went up to the fifth floor, then he unlocked their adjoining rooms and left, smiling at the size of the tip James gave him.

'Jean-Paul made the reservation,' James said in amusement, 'hold me absolved. I must admit I don't object to our being close together.'

He went ahead of her into her room, and Eleanor

followed him, exclaiming with delight. First there was a small but luxuriously appointed bathroom, then a large bedroom opening on to a living area where, joy of joys, louvred French windows gave on to one of the balconies. She stepped out on to it and gazed at the famous view in rapture, then giggled and called to James. He joined her quickly and followed her pointing finger, immediately beginning to laugh.

'I suppose you noticed the communicating door on your way through, complete with key, but what will you do about a communal balcony?'

'Pray you don't walk in your sleep!' Eleanor said tartly, and was rewarded with a light slap on her bottom.

'Come on,' ordered James, 'five minutes is all that you're allowed.'

As he left she flew into the bathroom and washed swiftly, touched up her face and flicked a brush over her hair. Feeling eager for her first Brazilian meal, she was ready when James tapped on the door and they went swiftly downstairs to look for Jean-Paul. He was sitting at a table near the end of the awning-covered terrace, a tall glass in front of him. He sprang to his feet as they arrived and installed Eleanor in her seat with ceremony, snapping his fingers for a waiter. In a very short time she was sipping a Campari and soda, and was immersed in the menu, which was in French and Portuguese.

Both men were amused at her indecision in the face of the enormous choice of food offered.

'Help me out. James,' she implored, 'you've been here before, what do you think I will like?'

James put down an outsize gin and tonic to lean close to study the menu.

Jean-Paul grinned at them wickedly.

'Keep your mind on the food, James! *Garçon!*' A waiter came hurrying over. '*O que é bom hoje*, Manoel?' '*A senhora gosta de peixe? A garoupa é gostosa hoje, com molho de camarão—uma delicia, Senhor Gérard.*'

Eleanor was decided.

'*Otimo,*' she said to the waiter, '*a garoupa para mim, por favor.*'

Jean-Paul gave an exaggerated double-take, looking at James in amazement.

'She looks like an angel and she speaks Portuguese as well. How talented!'

'Why else did you think I'd brought her?' said James drily. 'And use the word "accomplished", it's more graceful than "talented". My little paragon is inclined to violence if her unassailable virtue is in question.'

Eleanor frowned at him in disapproval, while Jean-Paul's dark, snapping eyes darted from one to the other with interest. Both men looked with pleasure at her absorbed face as she sat gazing avidly at everything in sight. The beach was a mass of brightly-coloured umbrellas, interspersed here and there with the inevitable football game beloved of all Brazilian male youth. Overhead in places great bird-like, vividly coloured kites hovered against the deep blue sky, suspended from strings held in the hands of their vendors.

When the waiter arrived with their lunch Eleanor's eyes opened wide. Anything less like her idea of fish in prawn sauce was difficult to imagine. Unlike its British counterpart, the sauce was almost a meal in itself. The crisply grilled fillet of thick white fish was masked in a steaming topping of prawns cooked with peppers, onions and tomatoes with garlic, served with small deep-fried potato balls. They all ate with gusto, discussing the arrangements made for the next few days. Eleanor was introduced to *vinho verde*, a sparkling

white wine, and listened to the other two while she ate
and drank, observing with interest the contrast the two
men made; Jean-Paul's darkness characteristically
Gallic, while James, though equally dark, still managed
to appear unmistakably British.

Both men regarded her plate reprovingly as she
finally abandoned it only half empty.

'*Me chère* Eleanor,' Jean-Paul wagged an admonishing finger, 'your shape is altogether delightful, you
have no need to make the *régime*—is it diet you say?'

'I'm sorry,' Eleanor sighed regretfully. 'There's
enough there for three, absolutely delicious, I admit,
but far too much.'

James took pity on her and changed the subject.

'By the way, Jean-Paul, I've been very remiss, I
haven't asked about Christiane. How is she?'

'Ah, my lovely Christiane.' Jean-Paul twirled his
wine-glass absently. 'She does not care for life here in
Rio. She was homesick for Paris, so she decided to
return *chez* Maman, at least for a little.'

Eleanor was surprised to see irony on James's face
rather than sympathy.

'Too bad, old son,' he murmured, rising. 'I think
this young lady is in need of a sleep this afternoon. I
think we'd better have a look at the site at Lagoã Azul
this afternoon, Jean-Paul, and leave Eleanor to have a
rest.'

As Eleanor rose she was only too glad to comply.
The large lunch as well as the wine, on top of her
sleepless flight, had left her almost dizzy with fatigue.
The two men escorted her to the lift and Jean-Paul
kissed her hand with éclat as he ushered her inside,
and her smile of farewell to James faltered before his
look of evident disapproval. Once in her room weariness enveloped her completely. She was barely able to

strip off dress and sandals before falling on the bed and fathoms deep into exhausted sleep.

She eventually surfaced to the sound of the phone ringing alongside the bed. The room was quite dark and she sat up muzzily to grope for the receiver. Her very blurred 'hello' met with an amused chuckle at the other end of the line.

'Rise and shine, sleepyhead—this is James, by the way.'

'Shame,' said Eleanor, finally locating the bedside lamp. 'I was hoping for Robert Redford.'

'I have it on good authority he can't make it tonight, so get yourself out of bed and into your party dress. I'll give you half an hour before I knock on your door, say nine-thirty.'

'Isn't that a bit late for dinner?' Eleanor stifled a yawn.

'Not in the least, it's early by Brazilian standards. See you later.'

Eleanor lay for five minutes, collecting her befuddled senses, then went into the bathroom and stood for some time under a lukewarm shower. Dried and scented, she quickly dressed in a sleeveless little slip of a dress in creamy pink shantung, blessing the gift of an olive-tinted skin so that her lack of tights would go unnoticed. A hint of violet eyeshadow, a flick of mascara and the lightest frosting of rose-pink lipstick were the work of a couple of minutes, then she brushed her hair thoroughly, braided it into a thick rope which she twisted into a coronet at the crown of her head, leaving some tendrils to twine in freedom above her ears. The expected knock came just as she was spraying herself again with 'J'ai Osé', and she gathered up her small clutch purse and went to open the door.

James was leaning indolently against the door jamb,

wearing a lightweight silver-grey suit worn with an open-necked maroon silk shirt. His eyes were appreciative as they took in her appearance.

'Not only Brazilian girls are delectable, princess. Your nap seems to have done wonders!' He locked the door behind her and led her to the lift.

'I was out for the count until you rang. I'd probably have slept until tomorrow if you'd left me,' admitted Eleanor.

James's smile was teasing.

'Perhaps I should have left you?'

Eleanor shook her head emphatically.

'I don't want to miss a minute of the time here in Rio, I can sleep when we return home. Is Jean-Paul dining with us?'

There was no answer from James as they arrived at the ground floor and entered the small but sumptuously appointed dining room. Two walls of the room were made of glass, which afforded the diners an uninterrupted view of the glittering jewelled curve of the Avenida Atlantica of Copacabana at night, complete with a moon shining down on the foam-edged sea.

A deferential major-domo led the way to a corner table, and James murmured into Eleanor's ear:

'I have a strong feeling that Betty Grable and Don Ameche will be at the next table, and any minute Carmen Miranda will come out and sing with the group that's playing over there—though I think they call it a *conjunto*, not a group. Or perhaps you're too young to remember those films.'

Eleanor chuckled as she sat down and was handed an enormous menu by one of the lesser waiters the major-domo had majestically summoned.

'I saw one on television only the other week.'

On James's advice she chose a Cuba Libre to drink,

which turned out to be Bacardi and Coca-cola, but with freshly pressed limes and a large quantity of ice, and they had read through a greater part of the complicated bi-lingual menu before James answered her question about Jean-Paul.

'Perhaps you're disappointed, but I discouraged friend Gérard from joining us this evening, much as he would have liked to. You made quite an impression there.'

Eleanor was sceptical.

'Nonsense! All that hand-kissing and complimentary bit is just his stock-in-trade—what everyone expects of a Frenchman.'

James held her eyes steadily.

'I thought you rather enjoyed it.'

'Of course I did, it was very entertaining, but hardly to be taken seriously. I'm not a complete dimwit, James.'

The warmth of her smile altered James's sober mood instantly.

'My apologies, princess. Now what shall we eat?'

He beckoned the major-domo, who spoke some English, and gave serious consideration to their choice. On his recommendation they started simply, with halves of avocado in vinaigrette sauce. The main dish he called *camaroẽs á grega*, which were enormous prawns curled round pearl onions wrapped in bacon and deep-fried in a delicious crisp batter, the finished result served on a bed of fried rice mixed with a variety of vegetables, some familiar, some not. The dessert was a chilled compôte of fresh figs served with crème Chantilly, and the whole washed down with quantities of red Brazilian wine which the major domo had described as being similar to the Dão wines of Portugal, full and smooth.

Eleanor sighed with repletion as she sipped strong black Brazilian coffee from a tiny cup. She looked dreamily at James, whose eyes were half-closed as they smiled back at her through the curling smoke of a cigar.

'I find it difficult to believe that we're here, actually here, in Rio, James. Seen through the window Copacabana looks unreal; do you think we could go for a stroll along the Avenida?'

He rose instantly, and they left the hotel to wander along a pavement paved with the now familiar mosaic, this time in wavy lines meant to represent the sea. Despite the lateness of the hour by British standards, the fabled Avenida was thronged with a gaily-dressed crowd enjoying the hot night and the slight salt breeze coming from the pounding surf-edged sea.

James held Eleanor's arm closely as they wandered along past hotels glittering with lights, music coming from many of them. Their steps became gradually slower and slower until James finally put his arm round her and gently turned her back in the direction of the Ouro Prato.

'Will you be ready to cope with our Brazilian gentlemen in the morning?' he asked.

'Of course. What time?'

'The manager is letting us use a room at the hotel for an office, and we shall make a start at nine, work through until about one. Lunch follows, than a short rest and work again from four to six. The evenings we have to ourselves, more or less.'

Eleanor smiled up at the dark face close to hers.

'Not much like a working day in the Midlands, is it?'

He touched his lips lightly to hers, regardless of passers-by. Eleanor's pulse quickened as his arm tightened round her, but their indolent pace had brought them back to the hotel, where he reluctantly disengaged himself to ask for their keys. The lift was empty, and they turned to each other simultaneously, his mouth coming down on hers with a tender intensity that made her tremble even as she pressed closer against him. The sudden stop of the elevator made them break apart to stare at each other dazedly before they walked hand in hand along the corridor to Eleanor's room. James opened her door and turned to her, handing her the key.

'Darling, I want very much to come in, but I won't even ask. Have no fear about the balcony either—no trespassing, I promise.'

Eleanor made a little sound halfway between a chuckle and a sob.

'Thank you, James, though why I'm thanking you is a bit obscure. Goodnight.'

She reached up and kissed his surprised mouth so swiftly that before his arms could automatically reach for her she was inside her room and alone, reproving herself sternly for wishing quite desperately she were not.

# CHAPTER SEVEN

THE sun woke Eleanor early next morning. It streamed through the louvred balcony doors, tempting her out to watch the early morning scene of Copacabana, which appeared not to have been to bed. She was showered and dressed in a sleeveless yellow cotton-knit shirt-waister before a smiling dark-skinned maid brought her breakfast. She ate at a small table set near the open windows, enjoying the strong black coffee laced liberally with cream, and crisp sweet rolls served with saltless butter and *marmelada,* a very sweet thick jelly made from quinces. At eight-thirty she opened the door in response to a light tap and found James smiling down at her, as summery as herself in white cotton slacks and shirt.

'Good morning—sleep well?'

'Very well—after a while,' added Eleanor truthfully. She gathered up notebook, pencils and handbag and went with James down to the second floor where he showed her into a large airy room furnished with a long table and several chairs, obviously used for meetings. As soon as Eleanor had arranged her belongings at the place next to James, Jean-Paul arrived with two men, the one quite young and slim, the other older and inclined to portliness. They were both swarthy-complexioned and black-haired, but the older man's was streaked with grey. Both were patently delighted to meet Eleanor.

'I am charmed, *senhora.*' The older man took her hand and raised it to his lips. 'José da Costa, *a seus ordems.*'

His English was a little laboured, with a strong American accent, and his eyebrows rose to his hair as Eleanor answered.

'*Eu tambem, senhor, muito prazer.* Eleanor Hunt.'

He broke into a flood of Portuguese, introducing his younger colleague as Helio Souza Lima, who added to the conversation, which Eleanor managed to follow with great concentration, leaving Jean-Paul to turn to James in amusement.

'A very wise move, James, to bring the so charming Eleanor. They eat out of her hand, as you say.'

'I suggest we get down to business,' said James briskly, and pulled out chairs for the Brazilians, Jean-Paul swift to establish Eleanor in hers with a flourish. The meeting progressed with great speed in an atmosphere of great cordiality, the two Latin gentlemen insisting on addressing Eleanor as 'Dona Helena', which pleased her greatly, and conferring with her constantly in Portuguese, while simultaneously dealing with James and Jean-Paul in English. Apart from a short break for coffee, they worked without stopping, to such good effect that at one o'clock it was decided that further progress had been made than thought possible, and the afternoon session was declared unnecessary.

Senhor José bent over Eleanor's hand and said earnestly, though in English for James's benefit:

'Now, Dona Helena, we must all lunch at Machado's farther along the *praia* at Posto Seis. Senhor Ramsay will allow if we present you with the delights of lobster eaten outside in the sun, watching all the *moças* go by in their *maillots*—how do you say, swimming costume.'

'Not that many of them ever swim in them,' put in Jean-Paul with a wicked grin. 'Strictly for the attraction of the male of the species!'

Eleanor ignored this sally, and looked at James enquiringly.

'It sounds the perfect idea, gentlemen,' he said
smoothly, ushering them out of the room. 'are you
coming too, Jean-Paul?'

'Frère Jacques, you could not keep me away!' The
black eyes were twinkling.

'I wouldn't mind trying,' said James, too softly for
the others to hear, 'and make no mistake, *mon brave*,
I'm no monk.'

Jean-Paul laughed delightedly and clapped James on
a reluctant shoulder as they followed the two men
escorting Eleanor downstairs.

It was decided they would stroll along to Machado's
in the hot noon sunlight, though the Brazilians were a
little anxious that Eleanor might find the sun too
powerful for her.

'Oh, please, gentlemen,' laughed Eleanor, 'I never
burn, and anyway there'll be precious little sun around
when we get back to England, not in December.'

It was not long before they were installed at one of
the outdoor tables at Machado's, glad to drink long
glasses of beer and nibble at the nuts and olives that
kept them occupied until the meal arrived. James was
just as impressed as Eleanor when the plates appeared,
each with half a lobster on the shell, served with an
enormous salad of every vegetable imaginable, including thick slices of a round white vegetable new to
Eleanor.

'How delicious! Senhor Helio, what is it?'

"*É palmito*, heart of palm. *Gostoso, nao é?*' He was
delighted at her obvious enjoyment.

'*Demais!*' she agreed fervently, 'and this mayonnaise
is superb. James, what are you so amused about?'

'I was just thinking that Mario's café in Market Square will be a bit of a comedown after all this.'

'Not a bit; that's home, and this is just a marvellous interlude.'

She smiled up at him, her eyes sparkling, and he leaned towards her involuntarily, but drew back as Jean-Paul broke in deliberately.

'James, José and Helio suggest that we all meet this evening and introduce you both to a *churrasco*. I do not think you visited one on the last trip.'

James was unable to do other than thank him for the invitation put in such a manner, smiling warmly at the Brazilians after looking at Eleanor for her approval.

'Just what is a *churrasco*?' asked Eleanor with interest.

'There's an open-air restaurant at the other end of Copacabana where all the meat is cooked over charcoal right in the middle of the room in full view of the diners. Whatever meat you choose is—ah—I think you say barbecued, impaled on a sword and slotted into a rack in front of your plate. You simply cut off pieces and eat them with various sauces, black beans, rice ...'

'Stop!' implored Eleanor. 'I shall have to sleep all afternoon to recover from this fantastic lunch, so that I shall be able to do justice to an equally fabled dinner.'

There was little need for concern, as apparently they would not be expected to meet until ten that night.

After they had parted company with the other three she and James wandered back to the hotel on foot.

'Did you mean what you said about wanting to sleep, Eleanor, or would you fancy lying under an umbrella on the beach for an hour or two instead?' James glanced at his watch. 'It's nearly four and the heat has subsided a bit.'

'Lovely! I was wondering when I'd get a chance to try for a tan.'

The hotel provided them with an umbrella and two straw mats to lie on, also they were shown a special elevator they could use if they decided to swim and wanted to return straight back into the hotel without changing.

Eleanor took a coral bikini and matching wrap-over skirt from her case, and was ready before James; who joined her in brief black swimming trunks with a towel flung over shoulders that were already bronzed. The elevator took them directly to the side of the building and they were quickly across the Avenida and settled on the beach on the straw mats, the umbrella shielding them from the full brilliance of the sun.

Eleanor smoothed oil over her arms and legs and lay on her back, head pillowed on her beach bag, and luxuriated in the warmth and sunlight. James lay motionless beside her and for some considerable time they drowsed in contentment, one of his long hands holding hers. Eventually Eleanor turned over. James reached for the bottle of oil and smoothed it over her shoulders and the back of her waist, moving down to her thighs with a rhythmic motion, running his fingers down to her ankles and then back again. Abruptly he stopped.

'That may have done nothing to you, but the effect on me was somewhat devastating.' His voice was muffled, just audible above the thunder of the sea.

Eleanor lay unmoving, then she turned her head sideways to look at him. He lay prone, his head on his arms.

'I didn't move away, James.'

'Do you think I didn't notice? Apart from the feel of

your skin it was your acceptance that made it damn difficult to move away. Good thing we're in a public place.' Still he lay face downwards.

Eleanor put out a tentative hand and touched his arm. Immediately he turned towards her and held her hand tightly.

He grinned at her crookedly, then his face grew serious.

'While we're alone, angel, may I make a small request?'

Eleanor smiled back at him indolently.

'Anything within reason.'

'I feel you're being a little too friendly to Jean-Paul, giving him a quite definite come-on, in fact. Would you please give him a stop signal? That roving Gallic eye is definitely turned in your direction, give him an inch, and you'll have a problem. Nothing so dangerous as a deserted husband on the loose!'

Eleanor lay perfectly still for so long, James almost believed she had heard nothing. Her euphoric mood of warmth and wellbeing was so completely dispelled she felt cold despite the heat of the afternoon. She rolled over on her back and sat up, taking a pair of large sunglasses from her bag and putting them on. She remained sitting, hugging her knees, staring out at the sea, her pleasure in the beautiful afternoon dissipated. There was an appreciable silence.

James sat up, his blue eyes wary.

'Aren't you going to say anything, Eleanor?'

She gave him a cool little smile.

'You know, I think I've had enough sun for the first time, unwise to overdo it. I'll go back to the hotel and take a leisurely bath. Please don't feel you have to come too.'

She stood up unhurriedly, wrapping her skirt round

her like a cape, then she left him sitting looking after her, his expression black.

When she arrived back in her room she felt almost sick with the iron control she had been exerting over her temper. She took several deep breaths to calm herself, looking at herself wryly in the mirror. For a few moments on the beach she had lain there beneath those tantalising hands, perfectly well aware that if they had been alone she would have turned into his arms and responded, undeterred by her customary reserve. The ill-timed request from James had damped her down like a cold sponge. Suddenly heat enveloped her whole body. Jean-Paul had been given no encouragement beyond the normal cordiality expected of an employee involved in James's gaining of the contract they had travelled such a long distance to secure.

Eleanor stripped off her bikini, rummaged in her suitcase for a paperback, then ran a lukewarm bath. She lay in it, forcing herself to concentrate on the novel. Gradually she relaxed and became interested in the plot. Eventually she washed her hair, and wrapping it turban-wise in a towel, she lay on the bed and drifted off into a doze.

As the night before the telephone woke her, but this time it was Jean-Paul's husky voice in her ear.

'*Bonsoir, chérie, ici* Jean-Paul. James is with you?'

'Good evening, Mr Gérard.' Her voice was cold. 'No, he is not.'

'Ah! *Pardon*. Will you tell me where he is? His room does not answer.'

'I have no idea. I haven't seen him since this afternoon.'

'*Non? Eh bien,* tell him that I shall be in the bar downstairs at nine-thirty. I will be chauffeur to take you to the Churrascaria Gaucho.'

'Thank you. Until later, then.'

Eleanor put the phone down, then jumped off the bed sharply as she saw how late it was. Three-quarters of an hour later she was bathed and dressed in her red silk dress, but decided it was too hot to wear the sequin jacket. The short spell in the sun had added a glow to her olive skin. In fact she looked rudely healthy, she thought, screwing gold studs into her earlobes. As it was still not completely dry her hair was twisted into an uncompromising knot on top of her head, its severity somewhat in keeping with her mood. When the expected knock came at the door she went to open it, uncertain how to greet James, but decision was wrested from her as he came in swiftly, kicking the door shut behind him. Before her indignant protest could leave her mouth he had seized her in his arms, kissing her savagely. For a few moments Eleanor was too surprised to struggle, but when the need for air became imperative she wrenched herself out of James's arms, breathing deeply, her eyes bright and cold with anger.

'Eleanor . . .' he began, frowning furiously.

'Good evening, James.' Eleanor spoke calmly and politely as though his onslaught had never occurred. James stood irresolute, his expression baffled.

'Jean-Paul rang earlier,' she went on. 'He was unable to find you, and for some reason imagined you might be here. He said he would wait for us downstairs at nine-thirty.' She glanced at her watch, then smiled at him coolly. 'It's a little more than that, so shall we join him?'

She picked up her purse and key, handed the latter to James and unhurriedly left the room. He followed her, locked the door and caught her by the arm as they waited for the lift.

'Forgive me, Eleanor, I didn't mean to attack you like that, but for God's sake say something about it—don't treat me as if I were non-existent!'

When the lift arrived Eleanor went in and leaned against the wall, contemplating him thoughtfully.

'I thought it best to ignore the whole thing, James. After all, it would hardly do for me to appear too encouraging.'

His face darkened.

'Ah, I see. You're still annoyed at what I said to you on the beach. Goddammit, Eleanor, I meant only that you should stop encouraging Jean-Paul. You don't need to freeze me off as well!'

'No doubt that's where I became confused.' Eleanor was all sweet reason. 'You see, I had no idea I'd been encouraging with anyone, just behaving with the normal courtesy to all three gentlemen I thought you would expect. However, no need for concern, I'll do my best to curb my natural friendly tendencies—to everyone.'

James was unable to say more as they arrived at the ground floor at that moment, and had perforce to follow her through the entrance lobby over to the bar, where Jean-Paul was already waiting.

'You're early,' said James coolly.

The Frenchman was lifting Eleanor's hand to his lips.

'I was most anxious to be on time. After all, the Brazilians still sometimes say 'hora Inglês' when asking for the punctuality, n'est-ce pas?'

Eleanor quickly suggested that they leave immediately for the Churrascaria Gaucho to meet the two Brazilians. A jolly drink together was obviously not on the cards, from the expression on James's face.

Later that night, back in her room, she prepared

wearily for bed. No one, she thought tiredly, could possibly say she was not pulling her weight on the trip. The meal had been superb, the Brazilians delighted at the way her eyes had widened when her *churrasco misto*, pieces of charcoal-grilled pork and beef, had arrived impaled on a sword which was set down with a flourish in a rack in front of her plate. She had tried manfully to keep up with the men in tackling such a large quantity of meat, but was relieved when the waiter took the sword away with half the meat uneaten. There had been great amusement from all the men when the waiter returned the sword to her only minutes later, the meat re-heated and ready for her to fall to again, much to Eleanor's dismay.

As the evening wore on more and more wine was consumed, and as both her Brazilian hosts abandoned all effort to speak English, they regaled Eleanor with details of their homes and families entirely in Portuguese. Her head began to ache with the effort of following their rapid colloquialisms, and conversing in another language all evening proved surprisingly draining, especially as she tried occasionally to hear what James and Jean-Paul were discussing. To her relief it appeared reasonably amicable; a very engrossing and technical conversation, and with one part of her brain she noted that Jean-Paul often lapsed into French which James appeared to have no difficulty in following.

It had been one-thirty in the morning before all four men accompanied Eleanor back to the hotel, where she was able to take a general leave of all of them, avoiding James's sardonic eye.

Morning came all too quickly, and in no time at all she was eating her breakfast and getting ready for the morning session. She had one fresh daytime dress left, a brown and white striped shirtwaister with a white collar, but as she battled with her mane of hair once more she seriously considered having it cut. At home it never seemed to be a problem, but here it was an extra chore to cope with in the midst of a crowded schedule. She abandoned all attempt to put it up and plaited it into a heavy rope while she waited for James to knock. It was nearly nine before he did. Eleanor was beginning to wonder if he had forgotten her and ran to open the door in relief.

'Good morning.'

He stood there unsmiling, relieved her of her key and conducted her to the conference room in silence apart from politely and perfunctorily enquiring if she had enjoyed her evening.

Eleanor was relieved to find the others already waiting for them, and after the usual civilities were exchanged they were soon plunged into what proved to be the final clearing up session. By noon all points had been settled, then everything would await James's report after he and Eleanor had returned to the U.K.

Senhor José and Senhor Helio pressed Eleanor to join them all for luncheon, as they would be unable to dine that evening. She smiled warmly at them both but declined, explaining, with what she hoped was tact, that the men would, she knew, like to be without feminine company for a farewell lunch, and she herself could not leave their beautiful country without buying presents for her family at home.

'You must eat something first.' James was quiet but firm.

'I'll have a sandwich sent up to my room,' she promised.

'Take a taxi into the city and visit the Rua Ouvidor. It's *the* place to shop in Rio, something like Bond Street in London, and if you don't take too long you can persuade the taxi driver to wait for you, or you'll never get back.' James took a roll of notes from his wallet. 'You'd better use Brazilian cruzeiros and pay me back later. In Sterling, of course.' His smile was crooked. They had fallen behind the others and were standing outside the lift. Eleanor looked at the money doubtfully.

'It seems a tremendous amount.'

'You'll need it. Be ready this evening by nineish—I believe Jean-Paul has some French restaurant in mind. Unlike last night you'll be able to talk English all evening. I appreciate your efforts very much.'

'Thank you, James.' Eleanor's smile was sincere as the lift doors opened. 'You're very kind.'

'I try, Eleanor. I bloody well try!'

The lift doors snapped shut on his moody face and Eleanor smiled to herself. She had the distinct feeling that the trip was turning out a little differently from the way James had intended.

# CHAPTER EIGHT

WHEN her sandwiches and coffee arrived Eleanor asked the waiter if he knew a hairdresser who would be likely to fit her in at a moment's notice.

'*Cabellereiro, senhora? Perfeitamente.*' The young man's smile was white in his dark face as he explained that his sister worked with the very expert hairdresser in the hotel, Senhor Antonio. If the Senhora would allow him to use the telephone?

The Senhora would, and after a rapid stream of Portuguese which Eleanor was only able to half-follow, he turned to her in triumph.

'Antonia *tem lugar numa meia hora, senhora. Isso servi?*'

An appointment in half an hour was infinitely more than Eleanor had hoped for, and to his delight she tipped the young waiter generously.

'*Sempre as seus ordems, senhora, muito obrigado.*' He bowed himself out happily.

Eleanor finished her lunch, made the necessary repairs to her face and hair and went down to the mezzanine where the hotel hairdresser's was situated. Senhor Antonio was a slender, elegant young man, ready to do everything he could to oblige the English lady, especially as she spoke his language so charmingly. After being shampooed by Maria-José, the waiter's sister, she was delivered into the hands of the master, who turned her face this way and that, spent some time in silent contemplation of her face, to Eleanor's amusement, then suggested she leave everything to him. When she was finally allowed to view the finished result in the mirror Eleanor felt transformed. A great deal of hair had been shorn off, and the remainder coaxed to curl round her head in layers of feathery fronds that just brushed her shoulders. The front had been cut to fringe her forehead softly, the whole hairdo moving with every breath. Eleanor felt lighter and younger—and frivolous, she decided. When Antonio had heard of her proposed shopping trip he instructed one of his girls to ring for a taxi owned by a friend, a very trustworthy driver, he assured her. The car was waiting outside when she emerged into the sunlight and she was soon on her way to the city of Rio, and the treasures of the Ouvidor.

When they arrived the taxi driver was quite happy to wait the specified hour Eleanor felt was necessary, both from a personal amiability and the fee that would be charged, but she felt justified in the expense, and after all the instructions had come from James.

The Rua Ouvidor proved to be very narrow, almost like an arcade, and Eleanor darted to and fro from one side to the other, unwilling to miss any of the beautiful things displayed. There were wood carvings, leather-work, ornaments in beaten copper, sparkling jewellery set with semi-precious stones as well as with diamonds and rubies. Eleanor forced herself to stop gazing and began to make her choices; a crocodile wallet for Richard, a white lawn dress embroidered in butterflies for Victoria and for each of the boys a hand-carved mule bearing panniers, all took suprisingly little time. After a pause she found a small exquisitely embroidered tea-cloth for Mrs Jenkins and then took a little longer to find something for Harriet. Eventually she decided on a charm for her gold bracelet, a *figa*, the national good luck charm of Brazil. The small clenched hand, perfect in every detail, was made of tortoiseshell, with gold fingernails and gold bracelets, guaranteed to keep the wearer safe from all harm.

There was still a little time before returning to pick up the taxi and Eleanor was by this time very thirsty, but as she was looking for somewhere to have a drink she caught sight of a very arresting shop window. Against a backdrop of flame-coloured satin was one dress; the only other thing in sight a black vase holding a great burst of orange zinnias. The dress was a slim strapless black silk sheath with over it a floating full overdress of white-dotted black organdie. Eleanor was suffused with longing. On impulse she went into the perfumed interior of the elegant shop and in no time at all the dress was removed from the window, tried on and pronounced '*um encanto*' by the pretty girl who helped her put it on. The 'enchanting' little dress cost her practically all of her traveller's cheques, and filled with guilt, she hurried back to the main Avenida and the spot where her taxi had arranged to wait for her. By the time the car had done battle with all the frenetic rush and bustle of Rio rush hour Eleanor was much later than she had intended in returning to Copacabana. When she entered the Ouro Prato the youth behind the reception desk handed her an evelope with her key. Inside was a short note in the familiar upright script. 'Gone to Lagoa Azul with J-P. We shall be in the American bar about nine. Come and meet us there. J.'

Eleanor went up to her room and laid down her packages, anxious to hang up her dress. Any feelings of guilt about her extravagance melted as she viewed it floating from its hanger on the wardrobe door. She suddenly caught sight of herself in the mirror and stood stock still in surprise. She had momentarily forgotten about the hair. I look quite unlike me, she thought, half regretful at the loss of the heavy mane. Harriet would be surprised. Eleanor went out on the balcony to look at the curving crescent of lights that were just beginning to bloom in the swiftly descending darkness. She marvelled that one minute there was a glorious sunset, practically the next minute the velvet dark came down like a jewelled mantle, studded with stars. Suddenly she caught sight of one of the kite-vendors packing up his wares on the mosaic pavement a little farther along from the hotel. Grabbing her purse and key, she ran to the lift and hurried out through the lobby. The little black-skinned vendor was just on the point of leaving, but was only too happy to sell her three of the exotic bird-shaped kites to take home for the boys. That must be the lot, Eleanor, she told herself sternly, as she bore her booty back to her room. You already owe James a fortune in sterling, so no more. But then who knew when she would ever be in such a glamorous place again?

Room Service obliged with a quite creditable pot of tea, though to Eleanor's surprise the milk served with it was piping hot. She sat appreciatively drinking several cups on the balcony, enjoying the beautiful panorama spread out before her, and listening to the everpresent muffled thunder of the surf. Tonight she was determined to take her time. The men could possess themselves in patience if she were a little outside the 'hora Ingles' Jean-Paul had called it. Despite her intention to linger as long as possible over her preparations, by nine-fifteen she was bathed, scented, made up with extreme care and examining her reflection in her clever, simple little dress. Although the under-slip was strapless the transparent overdress was high to the neck, secured there with a silk drawstring at the throat. The bias-cut spotted organdie floated sleeveless and loose, drifting free with every movement she made. The rather surprised Eleanor who looked back at her had undergone something of a metamorphosis. You mind you get home by twelve, Cinders, she giggled, picked up her small satin purse and went to join James and Jean-Paul.

Eleanor hesitated at the entrance to the bar, half concealed by an outsize rubber plant. The two men were deep in discussion, leaning against the bar. James looked darker-skinned than ever after his afternoon in the sun, the contrast emphasised by the off-white of the corded suit he had worn to Harriet's party. Beside him the smaller, wiry Frenchman gesticulated with animation to illustrate some point he was making, his elegance very much to the fore in a black jacket worn with white shirt and trousers. Eleanor saw James glance at his watch at least twice in quick succession, then he looked impatiently towards the doorway, his expression changing rapidly to one of warmth as he caught sight of her and came quickly across the small crowded room, a smile on his face which made Eleanor distinctly breathless.

'I had my hair cut,' she said unnecessarily, and smiled at him nervously. 'Do you like it?'

He took a deep breath.

'You look . . . I'm trying to find the relevant word, or perhaps there isn't one that precisely fits the picture you make. I'll just have to settle for enchanting, breathtaking, superb, stunning . . . just to name a few. Let's join Jean-Paul. What decided you to have your hair cut?'

Eleanor linked her arm gaily through his.

'Too hot, too heavy, too troublesome to cope with

and I suddenly felt like a complete change. Do you like it?'

'It's very fetching, but I'll miss that great rope hanging down your back like Pocahontas.'

As they joined Jean-Paul he took her hand to his lips with theatrical homage.

'Belle-Hélène, *comme vous êtes charmante*! What a triumph of a dress. Your afternoon was well spent, *n'est-ce pas?*'

Eleanor laughed ruefully, sipping the Campari and soda James handed her.

'You never said a truer word. Well spent is an apt description, I'm now destitute!' She turned eagerly to James. 'You should have seen the shops, they're sinfully tempting, and interesting too. I bought some terrific presents for the family, and I'm afraid the temptation was too strong when I saw this dress. I surrendered to it without the least resistance.'

'How uncharacteristic,' murmured James into his drink, then smiled at her mockingly. 'That dress was definitely not made to languish unseen, so after dinner I think we should take it dancing. I'm sure Jean-Paul will know a suitable *boîte*—nightclub to you, Eleanor.'

'*Mais oui*, that goes without saying, but first, *mes enfants*, let us proceed to Le Bec Fin, where the proprietor is a great friend of mine.'

The Frenchman ushered them out to his car and they were on their way to the other end of Copacabana, where in a very short time they were seated in a restaurant where the business of eating was something to be taken very seriously. They were installed in a booth on leather-topped benches at a table covered with a checked red and white cloth with candles set in plain glass-shaded holders. The menu was enormous, but handwritten, and everything, Jean-Paul assured them, was freshly cooked on the premises. After a great deal of consultation Eleanor chose smoked salmon to start, and the men had oysters *au naturel*. The main course was veal with sauce Madère followed by soufflé Grand Marnier, the whole washed down with quantities of superb claret.

'I know we should have had a white wine with the fish,' said Jean-Paul, grinning, 'but James is unshakeable in his devotion to red.'

Eleanor's face was demure as she finished her dessert.

'He has been known to drink white on occasion.'

'Ah, but that depends entirely on the occasion,' said James blandly, studying the contents of his glass.

The darting glance that Jean-Paul directed from one to the other was quizzical, then he rose as *le patron* came to ensure that all was well, and to offer them some very special Calvados to drink with their coffee. The atmosphere of conviviality was like a warm cloak shared by the three of them as they bade farewell and returned to Jean-Paul's car to drive the short distance to the *boîte*, Carlinho's, where they went down a steep flight of stairs to a small, dimly lit room, hot and crowded, where a three-piece *conjunto* of drums, piano and guitar played soft bossa-nova rhythms at the edge of a minute, packed dance floor.

James groaned as they settled themselves at a microscopic table near the bar, barely big enough to hold the three drinks Jean-Paul was ordering.

'I don't know that I'd be wise to drink anything else at all. Those Brazilians at Lagõa Azul this afternoon— my God, Eleanor, you should have tasted the drink they flattened me with. What did you call it, Jean-Paul?'

'Pinga, my friend. It consists of *cachaça*, a spirit

made from the sugar cane, very powerful, and they mix it with lemon juice and various other things. *Très fort!*'

Eleanor laughed. 'Did you drink it, Jean-Paul?'

'*Chérie*, I drink only wine. I found out long ago that for me this is the only way to survive. I must, of necessity, indulge in many business lunches and dinners, and very soon after I arrived in Rio I found survival possible by drinking the wine only. But tonight I will make exception. Here they achieve a whisky sour unrivalled anywhere.'

He called over a waiter and gave the order. Due to the size of the diminutive table their chairs were of necessity extremely close together. Eleanor was very conscious of the close proximity of James's thigh in deliberate warm contact with her own, and his arm negligently thrown across the back of her chair, just touching her shoulders.

'Did you enjoy your afternoon?'

His mouth grazed her ear, his breath warm on her neck as he spoke.

She sighed happily.

'Oh, James, it was wonderful, although I had the jitters about having my hair cut. I'm afraid I spent all your money too.'

'That's what I intended. Your hair looks and feels like shiny brown feathers; smells fascinating too.'

Jean-Paul turned to them as the drinks were brought, indulgently ignoring the little exchange.

'Now then, *mes amis*, try the drinks. Just for once I will forsake the grape for the grain; *délicieux*, you agree?'

Eleanor normally detested whisky, but she had to admit that the frost-rimmed glass of lemon flavoured spirit was very pleasant.

James regarded his glass doubtfully.

'This will probably be the last straw. You, of course, were sensible enough to avoid the *cachaça*, Jean-Paul.'

'Then sit here tranquilly while I dance with Hélène, for you must agree it is necessary to display the little dress that is so *ravissante*.'

James looked a little less than elated at the prospect, and watched moodily as the other two moved very slowly indeed on the over-congested, pocket-sized dance floor. Eleanor saw him order another drink from the waiter after quickly drinking the first, while she tried to dance as far from Jean-Paul as space would allow.

'You push me away, Belle-Hélène—are you afraid James will be jealous?'

'Annoyed, rather than jealous, I think. Which is the only reason for the exercise, isn't it? Ladling on all that Gallic charm! I have a strong suspicion that you speak English without much accent at all when you like, Jean-Paul. You really don't have to do all this Sacha Distel bit, you know, I'm quite immune.'

His eyes, that were so much more on her level than James's, shone wickedly before assuming an overdone air of innocence.

'But, Hélène, you are a very charming young lady. Also you have a little air about you, how shall I say, *un peu triste*, that makes men feel protective. Quite irresistible, I assure you.'

'Also quite unintentional, I assure you, but *merci du compliment, monsieur*, and I think James is looking *un peu triste* also. Let's go back to the table. Thank you for the dance.'

As they approached James rose immediately, took Eleanor by the hand and, without a word, led her back to the floor, where the *conjunto* was playing a slow, haunting little tune. They moved slowly, his arms round her in undisguised embrace, hers linked loosely behind his neck.

'I know the song, James, what is it?'

'A very old one, the theme from *Black Orpheus*, an old Brazilian film. Remember it?'

Eleanor nodded, then laid her head on his shoulder and surrendered herself to the music and his tightening embrace. There was a pause in the music and when she raised her face to his James said softly:

'I think it's time we went back to the hotel—it's late.'

When they arrived at the Ouro Prato Eleanor paused in the dimly-lit foyer and gave her hand to Jean-Paul, thanking him for the enjoyable evening. He kissed her hand, then looked in surprise as she turned and said goodnight to James in turn. The latter's eyes narrowed, his face instantly stony.

'Goodnight, Eleanor.' His voice was sardonic. 'Don't forget Jean-Paul is picking us up at six.'

Promising to be on time, Eleanor walked to the open lift, waving a hand insouciantly to the watching men as the doors closed behind her. She smiled mischievously to herself as she let herself into her room; not for anything would she have allowed James to come up with her in the lift in the face of the expression of those world-weary French eyes.

She hung up her dress with loving care and went through the evening dreamily in her mind as she prepared indolently for bed. Tonight at least there had been fewer undercurrents, and she had enjoyed herself very much, despite Jean-Paul's unwanted attentions, which, she well knew, were designed to irritate James rather than to charm herself, and they were only too successful. After her shower she decided to pack up the presents, then shrugged and thought she might as well pack her clothes as well. She had almost finished when a very quiet knock at the door made her spin round, stiffening. The knock was repeated. Eleanor went to the door and asked cautiously who was there.

'*C'est moi*—Jean-Paul. A moment, please, Eleanor.'

Surprised, she opened the door reluctantly, and he pushed past her smiling at her air of disapproval.

'Do not look so suspicious, *chérie*.' He produced her small evening purse and brandished it. 'I found this when I got back to the car.'

'How kind of you to return it.' Eleanor was coolly formal. 'You could easily have left it at the desk downstairs, or given it to me in the morning.'

His face was innocent.

'But there might have been something very necessary to you in it, *n'est-ce pas? Eh bien*, give me a little kiss as a reward and I will depart.'

Eleanor felt icily furious.

'For heaven's sake, Jean-Paul, there's no one here to perform for now. Thank you for the bag; just go now, will you, please.'

To her horror he made no move to go, but seated himself on the arm of one of the chairs, swinging a leg casually.

'After all, *chère*,' he said airily, 'Christiane, my wife, she liked so much your strong, silent James. She found him very attractive indeed, and did very little to conceal the fact. I did not care for that at all. I think it only fair—and you know how much you British love the justice—that I should steal just one little kiss from his *chère-amie* by way of reparation.'

He lunged suddenly from the chair and caught her by the upper arms, bending his head to hers, but before he could get any further an iron hand had plucked Eleanor from Jean-Paul's grasp and she looked up in dismay, an icy sensation in the pit of her stomach. James had obviously come in by way of the balcony, and was wearing what appeared to be solely a knee-length towelling robe. His face bleak with rage he took a menacing step towards the Frenchman.

'Get out, Jean-Paul, before I'm overtaken by the urge to assist you with my fist!'

The other man threw up his hands gracefully, his knowing glance travelling deliberately from James's robe to Eleanor's filmy green lawn wrap.

'*Milles pardons*. I did not expect to find myself so very much *de trop*. Sleep well, *mes enfants*. *À demain*!'

With a mocking bow he left, closing the door behind him with exaggerated care.

There was a highly unpleasant silence in the room after his departure. Eleanor looked cautiously up at James, prepared to defend her unwilling part in the embarrassing little incident, when she realised with a growing feeling of alarm that James was not perfectly steady on his feet as he glared down at her. In fact, it was very obvious that he was very definitely far from sober. She swept into the attack.

'I could very well have got rid of my uninvited visitor unaided. Why on earth did you erupt into my bedroom so dramatically?'

'It seemed to be open house as far as I could tell,' he drawled sneeringly. 'I was on the balcony, enjoying some fresh air before turning in, when I heard voices. I felt obliged to investigate in case something was wrong. Forgive me if I interrupted a prearranged assignation.'

'Oh, stop talking like someone out of a Regency romance!' Eleanor snapped. 'Now, if you don't mind, I'd like to go to bed.'

'I don't think I should leave you disappointed,

"*chérie*".' The tone of his voice made Eleanor squirm.
'After all, if you were in the mood for a little dalliance
I'm more than happy to serve as substitute.'

Eleanor backed away from him in disbelief, her eyes
wide with apprehension as they stared into his, but
with one sudden unsteady lunge he trapped her in arms
which were transformed into iron bands as a relentless,
vengeful mouth descended on hers.

Eleanor began to twist and struggle in deadly earnest, the beginning of a very real fear overtaking her.
She pushed in vain at the hard chest, appalled at the
mirthless chuckle deep in his throat, and threshed
wildly in his unrelenting grip, gaining a second's re-
spite only to hear a tearing sound as the front of her
flimsy dressing gown ripped in his grasp. She gave a
little moan of despair as he negligently captured both
her hands in one of his and divested her of the remains
of her wrap with the other.

'James, please!' she begged, repelled by the heat and
desire that turned his eyes into molten blue slits.

'What are you pleading for, my lovely?' The deep
voice had lost its smoothness and had a breathless rasp
as he pulled her hard against him. A fog of alcohol and
jealous rage had stripped away the cultured veneer to
change him into a menacing stranger. 'I'm not taking
any more of this blow hot, blow cold treatment,
deliberately baiting me with that bloody Frenchman.
Now I'm calling the tune.'

'James . . .' Eleanor made a last despairing bid to
reason with him, but he was past heeding anything but
the urgency in his own body, and the feel of hers trembling against him. His mouth silenced her abruptly as his
hands caressed and roamed restlessly over curves only
partly concealed by her very brief lawn nightdress.

A voice in Eleanor's brain was repeating dully:

'Not like this, please not like this!' But he had lifted her and carried her unsteadily over to the bed, where he laid her ungently down. In an instant she rolled to the other side, but a detaining hand caught her shoulder and turned her roughly towards him. Two insultingly casual fingers hooked into the front of her nightdress and tore it deliberately to the hem, casting aside the tattered remains while one hand held both of hers above her head. For a long breathless moment he gazed down at what he had, his face a darkly flushed mask of blind desire, his breathing ragged and irregular. Blind to the entreaty in her eyes, his mouth came down again on hers, his hands releasing her to caress the trembling reluctant body before covering it with his own.

This can't really be happening, thought Eleanor, frantic with despair. The agony of the whole thing was that her traitorous body wanted quite violently to respond to the cavalier treatment it was receiving, to thrust itself even closer to the persuasive body bent on its possession. But as a hard thigh sought to part hers she gave one instinctive frantic heave upwards, taking him by surprise in his absorption. In the struggle that followed there was a sudden horrendous creaking, rending noise, and the bed slowly collapsed in ruins beneath them. For one moment they lay in appalled silence, then Eleanor leapt from the ruins of the bed and dived for the remnants of her dressing gown, wrapping it fiercely round her as she rounded on James, who was tying the sash of his dressing gown and regarding the wreckage with a very odd expression on his face. Unlike its British counterpart, this bed consisted of a mattress supported on wooden slats held by a wooden frame, with a headboard and footboard. The structure had disintegrated beneath the rough treatment it had received.

Sobriety had obviously returned to James instantly and completely. To Eleanor's wrath his shoulders began to shake and he was convulsed with helpless laughter, the tears streaming down his face.

'I do hope you will not consider me lacking in courtesy if I don't share your hilarity.' Eleanor's voice was icy. 'Perhaps you would now be good enough to return to your own room and stay there for what's left of the night.'

James controlled himself with a heroic effort and turned his attention from the bed, the mirth fading from his eyes as he took in the torn dressing gown she was struggling to keep in place. He thrust a hand through his hair, looking at her warily.

'I don't quite know where to begin to apologise, Eleanor. To begin with, I'm sorry about wrecking your—er—your clothes—I'll replace them, of course.'

'Oh, don't apologise to me,' said Eleanor bitterly. 'It's Harriet you can grovel to, she lent them to me.'

'God!'

'There's not much point in getting religion at this stage. Now will you please leave? Right now.'

'Look, Eleanor, you go and sleep in my bed and I'll camp out on one of those settees.'

Eleanor's look would have withered a blossoming tree at six paces.

'Do you think I'm an imbecile? Just get back where you belong and *I'll* sleep on the settee—not that I expect to do much sleeping. I shall be far too occupied in trying to dredge up sufficient Portuguese to explain what could possibly have happened to that accursed bed.'

James headed for the window leading out to the balcony. He turned before he reached it, his face deliberately apologetic.

'If you revile that bed so violently, darling, I shall begin to think you regret it collapsed when it did.'

Eleanor stood with eyes closed and fists clenched for several seconds after James's departure. Her head and body seemed in equal turmoil. Confound all men, she thought savagely, throwing pillows and a sheet on the settee. Never again, if she could help it. This comforting thought was strangely not nearly as conducive to sleep as it should have been.

# CHAPTER NINE

THE flight home next day was something Eleanor preferred to forget. By a stroke of good luck, at least as far as she was concerned, the plane was full and there was no possibility of sitting next to James. Once they were airborne she lay back in her seat, eyes closed, exhausted by all the drama of explaining the broken bed, first to a wide-eyed maid and then to the suave manager. The journey to the airport afterwards had been accomplished in total silence on her part, though to her chagrin James and Jean-Paul had chatted desultorily as though the awkward little incident of the night before had never occurred. All overtures made to her by James had been met with chill uninterest, until finally by the time their flight had been called he had relapsed into silence as complete as hers.

They arrived late on Saturday evening to a chill wet British November drizzle. Eleanor shivered as they went through Customs, and by the time they had endured the inevitable wait for luggage and were at long last installed in the Porsche she was chilled in every bone. James tossed a rug on her lap and, without comment, she huddled into it as they made their way through the tunnel and out of the airport, to head for the M4 and the Midlands.

Beyond asking if she were warm enough James made no attempt at conversation. Eleanor was thankful, but sat miserably as the powerful car ate up the miles, wanting only a warm bed and oblivion. She had a splitting headache and a strong suspicion that a cold was imminent. You should have stayed at home, she told herself morosely, looking up at James's uncompromising profile. After asking her where she wanted to be dropped James eventually stopped the car in Mill Crescent, helped her out punctiliously, and carried her suitcase to the door. Eleanor trailed behind, clutching the bag full of kites, feeling somewhat ridiculous. James took her key and put it in the lock, then looked down at her.

'I imagine there's no earthly use in my starting to apologise all over again for my behaviour last night.' His voice was abrupt. 'I wasn't entirely in command of myself, but I'm aware that is a feeble excuse.'

'Let's forget the whole thing.' Eleanor was acutely embarrassed. 'Erase it from the records.'

He bent slightly, as if to kiss her, but straightened sharply at her involuntary withdrawal.

'There's not really much more to be said, then, Eleanor. I'll see you on Monday morning.'

She nodded dumbly, then opened the door and went in. Mrs Jenkins emerged from the back of the house as the front door closed, exclaiming as she saw Eleanor's face.

'How weary you look, love—did you have a good time? I think you've caught the sun a bit; tiring trip, was it?'

Eleanor let herself be fussed over, sitting gratefully in her landlady's kitchen while she was fed with soup, scrambled eggs and lots of strong tea, until eventually she handed over the tablecloth she had brought for Mrs Jenkins and wished her goodnight. In her flat she only stopped to heat water for a hot-water bottle before falling into her bed to seek comfort in oblivion, in spite of an unwelcome voice in her head which kept telling her what a witless idiot she was not to have let James do what he wanted the night before. She burned at the thought that she had undeniably wanted it too. As she lay willing sleep to overtake her Andrew Marvell's lines kept running round in her head: 'The grave's a fine and private place, but none I think do there embrace.'

Eleanor went over to Tollmarston the next morning to distribute her presents to their ecstatic recipients, and managed to avoid being alone with Harriet, as far as possible. After one sharp perceptive look her sister, with great forbearance, forbore to probe any deeper into Eleanor's air of malaise, beyond demanding an account of the trip and exclaiming over the haircut. The now fully developed cold served as a splendid excuse for Eleanor to return home early. A tactful Richard drove her home and merely gave her some professional advice as to the treatment of her cold. Surprisingly he gave her a quick hug before leaving, and with a lump in her throat, Eleanor obediently took some pills and a hot drink, then retired to sweat out her misery, physical and mental.

By the time she arrived at Ramsay & Coulter on Monday morning she was in a cold panic at the thought of facing James. She had half hoped, half feared, he might be waiting to pick her up, but no powerful black car was at the gate when she went out into Mill Crescent. Everyone was full of enthusiasm at how brown she looked on her arrival in reception, and her hair attracted a lot of attention. Louise at the desk sighed in envy at the thought of such a glamorous trip and refused to be damped down when she heard Eleanor sneezing. Frances was waiting in her office and went through the same routine, except that her keener eye noted the shadows beneath Eleanor's.

'Had a hectic time, I see. Hope you're not expecting

any sympathy after living it up in foreign parts! Was it fantastic?'

Eleanor smiled wanly.

'It was indeed, and now I have the sniffles by way of recompense. I hope you weren't frantically over-worked, Frances.'

'Not a bit of it,' said Frances cheerfully. 'There's a certain amount I had to leave for you, otherwise it wasn't too bad. Well, must press on, I suppose—see you later.'

Eleanor made a determined effort to immerse herself in her usual routine, fingers mechanically opening and sorting the post, but ears constantly alert for the sound of the buzzer or for any movement from the next office. It was difficult to keep her eyes from straying to the communicating door, and her stomach lurched when this finally opened, but it was Hector Ramsay who stood there, smiling genially. Torn between relief and disappointment, Eleanor sprang to her feet, hand out-stretched.

'Mr Ramsay! How lovely to see you, and looking in such obvious good shape, too.'

'Hello, my dear.' He took the hand and held it, look-ing down at her searchingly. 'Wish I could say the same for you. You're browner, I suppose, from all that South American sun, but you're skinnier, lass, not to mention the dark circles under your eyes.'

Eleanor coloured under his probing look and smiled evasively.

'Coming down to earth to the British climate has given me rather a messy cold, that's all. And of course, it was a hectic few days in Rio, although I'm sure you must be pleased with the outcome.'

'As far as the hotel project is concerned it was very good news. But with James about as happy as a caged lion, and you looking like a little suntanned ghost, there must have been something not so right somewhere.' Hector looked at her speculatively. 'Margaret thought I'd better come in and see for myself. No need to keep looking over your shoulder like a nervous mare—James had to leave for London early this morning. He's needed down there for a day or two. What's the matter, Eleanor? I rather had the impression you and James were hitting it off quite well after a stiffish start.'

'Nothing at all, really. Just jet lag and unaccustomed high living for me, I suspect, though of course I can't answer for James.' Liar, she thought secretly. 'Are you staying to help me out today, Mr Ramsay?'

'No fear! Margaret has allowed me off the leash for one hour precisely, she said. Watches me like a hawk; don't you think I've lost weight?' He patted his stomach smugly. 'Heavy on the lettuce and light on the potatoes is her motto. Works, though, I must admit.'

'You look terrific,' said Eleanor sincerely, 'and a great advertisement for Mrs Ramsay's care and attention. Give her my love.'

'That sounds very politely like marching orders, lass.' Hector's eyes, so like his son's, twinkled down at her. 'I know you've a lot to get on with, and I'll be very interested to read the Brazilian report once James has had a look at it. Now, miss, take care of that cold.'

With a wave of his large hand, Hector Ramsay departed, leaving Eleanor to plunge into the work awaiting her, almost lightheaded from the relief of avoiding confrontation with James, at least for the time being.

The next few days went by in a haze of hard work, aching head, violent sneezing and sleepless nights due in part to blocked sinuses, but mainly due to incessant heartache over James. During the day she was able to keep this at bay in the press of work, except that every time her phone rang she answered it in eager expectation of hearing the familiar deep voice on the line. James remained ominously quiet, however, and she grew more and more miserable as the week drew on, her appetite practically non-existent.

Mrs Jenkins was very concerned, and insisted on doing Eleanor's shopping and making hot lemon drinks. Harriet rang up every evening begging her to stay home from work and take to her bed, and much as she would like to have given in and complied, Eleanor was determined to have the Brazilian report completed as well as the routine things that she was able to see to independently. She worked doggedly on, and by Thursday morning the worst of the cold had cleared up, but it left her listless and disinclined to eat. She was unable to face more than a cup of coffee before leaving for the office, and at lunchtime she resolutely refused all Frances's blandishments regarding food. A cup of tea and a plain biscuit eaten in solitude at her desk were as much as she could manage, but she went home that evening with the rough draft of the Brazilian report finally ready for James whenever he chose to reappear, and a feeling of definite achievement.

Before she reached the flat Eleanor's whole aim in life had been to collapse on her sofa with a mug of soup and a sandwich in front of the most mindless programme on the television she could find. Yet when she had discarded her outdoor clothes she became oddly possessed of a feeling of unrest, and in no mood to put her feet up after all. Changed into old cord jeans and a tee-shirt, she decided to work up an appetite by washing the kitchen walls, a chore she had been postponing for some time. Eleanor went downstairs to borrow a ladder from a highly disapproving Mrs Jenkins and set to with a will, up to her elbows in suds.

For a while the vigorous rubbing and rinsing counteracted the restless feeling, but Eleanor very soon found it left her mind free to run on its familiar track, round and round and round, like a record with the needle eternally stuck.

It's no use, she thought despondently, whatever I do it all comes back to James, James, James, just like a schoolgirl with her first crush. Perhaps that was the root of the problem. The type of normal, healthy teenage crush that is the prerogative of most girls had never really occurred for her. Nick had been a childhood companion who had made a natural progression into sweetheart. There had been none of the agonising and soul-searching that most of her companions in college seemed to regard as a necessary part of life. Her own life had been wrenched apart at a time when the average girl was usually coming into the full bloom of sexual awareness. Bleak adulthood had arrived in one fell swoop, and all her natural instincts had been repressed by the overwhelming fear of exposing herself ever again to the risk of being hurt.

Eleanor refilled the bucket with clean soapy water and remounted the ladder to attack the ceiling. It was hard to believe that only one short month ago her life had been an ordered and well-regulated affair, troubled by few emotions other than the love and affection channelled towards Harriet and her family. James Ramsay had merely been the name of her employer's son. I wish it had stayed that way, she thought bitterly, climbing down the ladder and moving it on to a new section of ceiling. What I used to pride myself on as my poise and self-possession must have been plain cowardice; just fear of letting anyone near enough to penetrate the barrier it took six years to build. James demolished it the first moment I set eyes on him. Oh, blast!

Eleanor swore inelegantly as soapy water sloshed in her eye after a particularly vicious wring of the wash-cloth. Enough was enough. She put her bucket away, spread the cloth to dry and redirected her thoughts to eating. Presumably I will enjoy eating again sometime, she thought listlessly, and inspected the contents of the fridge with distaste. One consolation was the thought of the Brazilian report ready and waiting for James's return, when and if he did. Eleanor froze. A disquieting thought had just occurred to her.

All confidential documents were locked away at night at Ramsay & Coulter's, the one currently being worked on usually locked up in a special drawer in her desk. Eleanor's mind was blank as to what she had done with the Brazilian report, and she had a sinking feeling it might have been left out in full view. She thought frantically, but the more she racked her brains the less sure she became. Finally she sighed in ex-asperation and dragged a hairbrush through her hair and put on a shiny red waterproof jacket. She tele-phoned for a taxi and went downstairs with the ladder to tell Mrs Jenkins where she was going. When the taxi deposited her in Westgate Street Eleanor let her-self into the dark office building feeling decidedly ill at ease. When it was crowded during the daytime the antiquity of the building was not so much in evidence as now when it was dark and deserted. As she tiptoed up the stairs, only one light on to see her way, she was very conscious that this had once been a great house, peopled with human beings, all with problems and emotions like her own.

Giving herself a little shake, she reached her office and switched on the gooseneck lamp on her desk. All her desk drawers were locked, as usual, and when she opened the one reserved for important documents, there was the Brazilian report, safe and sound. Eleanor locked it again in vexation, cursing herself for being all kinds of a fool, and put out a hand to switch off the desk light. A slight sound from the doorway made her stiffen and spin round. A shadowy figure stood in the dimly-lit doorway. She gave a hoarse little cry as all the blood seemed to drain from her body and she fainted dead away.

When Eleanor slowly opened her eyes the only thing in her vision was James's face bent over her own in an agony of anxiety. At the unguarded look of joy in her eyes, he took a deep, unsteady breath and involuntarily bent his mouth to hers.

'What in hell's name are you doing her at this hour?' he muttered lovingly against her lips. 'I thought you were breaking and entering.'

'James . . .' she said faintly, 'I can't breathe.'

'Sweetheart, I'm sorry.' He relaxed his hold a fraction. 'Don't ever do that again, you frightened the living daylights out of me!'

Eleanor struggled feebly in his hold.

'*I* frightened *you*?' she said indignantly. 'I thought you were a ghost or a burglar; I don't know which frightened me more. I've a notion I'm supposed to ask "Where am I?"'

James shifted a little, settling her more comfortably.

'You're lying across my lap. I'm sitting on the floor with my back against your desk and I'm holding you in my arms.'

'How succinct. I'd gathered that. Why are we sitting on the floor?—and I thought you were still in London.'

'I caught you very neatly as you fell and we somehow

landed this way. As far as my sudden return from the Metropolis is concerned, I worked like the maniac some people consider me,' he paused, looking down at her significantly, 'so that I could get back here as soon as humanly possible. Now then, up you get and let's see if you can stand all by yourself.'

He eased her off his lap and stood up, then held out his hands to pull her up. Eleanor's legs felt like cotton wool, but her head stopped revolving quite quickly once she was as upright as it is possible to be when held firmly against someone's chest.

'You can let me go now, James,' she said indistinctly. 'I'm perfectly all right now, I think.'

'Possibly, but I'm retaining my hold on you for the time being, while you're too fragile to fight. Do you often faint?'

'This is the first time, though it's not really a mystery as to why. I haven't eaten anything much all day, and for the past few days really.'

James shook her slightly.

'Why in heaven's name not?'

'Since we—since we came back from Rio I've had rather a heavy cold, and consequently I haven't felt hungry.' Eleanor drew rather a shaky breath. 'My sinuses hurt and I couldn't get to sleep and—and—oh, James!' To her horror she began to sob wildly into his jacket. 'I've been so miserable this week!' She wailed like a child.

Holding her closely with one arm, James fished his other hand into his breast pocket and took out a handkerchief, mopping her up as best he could while the stream of tears continued unchecked.

'Darling, please, don't cry like that or you'll have me joining in.' He tried to keep his tone light. 'I've been just as wretched as you. More so, I imagine, as I thought you'd never forgive me for going berserk in Rio. I've called myself every name under the sun, most of which I won't repeat to your sheltered ears, and kicked myself metaphorically from here to London. Is it remotely possible that I'm forgiven?'

Eleanor's sobs gradually died away and, to James's surprise, he heard a weak little chuckle coming from the region of his saturated silk tie. He turned her face up to his.

'What's so amusing?'

'It wasn't really the rape and pillage bit that upset me so much, James, it was having to explain about that beastly bed!'

He grinned wickedly down at her.

'The manager spoke English perfectly well. He didn't turn a hair when I told him to add the damage to the bill—duly itemised. After all, Jean-Paul was footing the hotel bill, I thought it might make him wonder a bit.'

They leaned against each other laughing helplessly, until the humour died out of James's face and he bent to kiss Eleanor's unresisting mouth. Her arms went round him convulsively, and they clung together in the heady relief of reconciliation. After a lengthy interval he loosened his hold slightly.

'As you're literally fainting with hunger, Eleanor, I'm taking you home for a meal.'

'James! I can't possibly go anywhere looking like this. I was washing the kitchen walls when I suddenly thought I hadn't locked away the Brazilian report.'

'So that's why you were here—I was sidetracked from my original query.' James smiled at her possessively. 'It doesn't matter a damn what you look like. Your eyes are red, your nose is shining, your mouth looks as if it's been kissed to death, and if we don't go right this instant I warn you I shall take up where I left off in Rio!'

Eleanor was filled with rapture at this complimentary statement and smiled back at him dreamily as she buttoned up her waterproof jacket.

'Very well, James, I'll do whatever you want.'

He looked down at her sharply, his eyes disbelieving.

'You sound as though you mean what you just said.'

'I do,' said Eleanor simply, and held out her hand.

James took a deep breath and took it, leading her swiftly out of the office, switching off lights as they went. Eleanor floated down the stairs in a happy daze, her cold forgotten, content just to feel his hard, warm hand holding hers and to relish the feeling that her world had righted itself again. The realisation filled her suddenly. James was the pivot on which her world revolved, and there seemed very little point in trying to conceal the fact any longer, certainly no more self-deceit was any use. As if he sensed what she was thinking James paused as they crossed the shadowy hall.

'What is it, my darling?' he said softly.

Her habitual reserve made Eleanor disinclined to lay her heart bare without time to consider this new discovery, so she smiled shyly.

'I was thinking how quickly my cold seems to have disappeared since I fainted, not that I suppose the two are connected.'

James locked the outer door after them and led her to the car rapidly in the pouring rain. He settled her in the Porsche and switched on the ignition.

'I would very much like to think there was a less prosaic reason for your recovery.' He said, keeping his eyes on the road as he drove off. 'I must be honest and say I can hardly credit this sudden submission. You're quite sure you feel completely well?'

Eleanor smiled serenely as she looked out in contentment at the teeming rain dancing in the beam of the headlights.

'I'm just glad to see you, that's all. I thought you would ring me while you were in London, but I expect you were too busy.'

'I started to a hundred times. I even dialled your flat once, but I put the phone down before it could ring. I was in a funk at the thought of hearing that icy uninterest in your voice, so I left it until I could try a more personal approach. God, what a bloody awful week it's been!' James's voice was so heartfelt Eleanor thought she might as well be honest.

'Every time the phone rang I hoped it was you,' she said very quietly.

James looked sideways at her bent head, then she heard him laugh softly.

'Oh, what fools we mortals be!' His hand reached out and covered her knee. 'Old Will wrote a lot of good sense, my love. There's another bit, very applicable, different play. How about "Come kiss me, sweet and twenty, youth's a stuff will not endure."'

'Apart from the fact that I'm just a bit more than twenty,' said Eleanor demurely, keeping her eyes ahead, 'I think he definitely had the right idea. I wholeheartedly approve.'

'I notice you choose to say something provocative like that when I can do nothing about it.'

Eleanor changed the subject hurriedly, to his amusement.

'How did you happen to be passing the offices at that moment? It can hardly be on your route home from the motorway.'

'When I come back from a trip I usually have a meal with Mother and Dad,' he said obliquely. 'But I rang and cried off for this evening, as I had something of pressing importance to attend to. *Ergo*, I came straight through town to see you before going home; I intended to present myself on your doorstep so that you could hardly refuse to see me. I was afraid to ring first in case you hung up. As I came through Westgate Street I saw a light and thought I'd better investigate. Here we are.'

He brought the car to a stop, jumped out into the still heavy rain and ran round to let Eleanor out.

It was too wet and dark for her to see much of the outside of the cottage, which fronted directly on to the uneven pavement, but as James hurriedly unlocked the door and ushered her inside she stood still and took a deep breath of pure appreciation as he turned on the lights and she was able to see the interior.

The inner partitions of the cottage had been knocked down to form the ground floor into one large living area, with the roughcast walls painted white to contrast with the darkness of the original beams in the ceiling. The floor was covered in a plain tweed-like carpet in a warm burnt orange, just a shade or two darker than the heavy velvet curtains. At one end of the room a hearth in honey-coloured Cotswold stone held an iron brazier full of gas logs that leapt into life at the touch of a switch, looking remarkably life-like as they crackled beneath a cowled copper hood. Either side of the fireplace were two alcoves, each with a small window and a set of shelves. At the back of the room was a larger window beneath which stood a leather-topped desk furnished with a workmanlike lamp, and was obviously James's working area. In front of the fireplace two squashy brown leather settees faced each other, a low round leather-topped table between them.

Eleanor surrendered her jacket to James in silence, still looking round her with absorption. The original staircase had been removed, and a wrought-iron spiral stair now gave access to the upper floor. Beyond the stair a trellised wood screen partially divided the living room from a small kitchen and dining area.

'Well,' James prompted, 'what do you think of it?'

Eleanor's eyes shone with enthusiasm.

'I had no idea it would be anything like this, James. I'd imagined beams, of course, but with brass and chintz everywhere.'

He grinned wryly.

'There were. Erica had it looking very olde-worlde, with the original partitions and brass bits and pieces everywhere, chintz-covered furniture and matching curtains, even a flowered carpet. I decided to get rid of the lot and do my own thing. You approve?'

'How could I not! Is it divided in the same way up-stairs too?'

'More or less. There was a small boxroom over roughly the kitchen area, and this is now the bathroom. The bedroom I had knocked from two smaller ones—not that I'm offering to show you over it, our experiences in bedrooms hasn't been too happy to date.'

Eleanor chuckled.

'Let's investigate the kitchen instead. Are you likely to have anything to eat?'

They looked through the fridge, to find Mrs Ramsay had filled it to capacity. There were slices of rare roast beef, a joint of ham, a bowl of ready-mixed salad and another of cold cooked potatoes.

James regarded these perplexed and looked at Eleanor.

'What do you think Mother intended me to do with these?'

Eleanor took them from him, laughing.

'What a helpless male! Give me a frying pan and I'll sauté them.' She inspected the contents of a pan on the cooker. 'There's some very tempting-looking soup in this—French onion. You lay the table while I see to this lot—some cheese I can grate, please.'

In double-quick time they were tucking into what seemed to Eleanor the best meal she had ever had. James produced crusty bread, a bottle of claret, and on further inspection the fridge had yielded up one of Mrs Ramsay's blackberry pies for dessert.

They sat together as close as possible on the padded bench at the small pine table, the conversation flowing free and fast as James described his week in London and brought himself up to date on matters at the Midland office, and Eleanor's progress on the Brazilian report.

Eventually Eleanor sat back, replete. James looked at her indulgently as she patted her stomach.

'Feeling better now?'

'That was, without exception, the most delicious dinner of my entire life, James. Thank you very much, I had no idea I was so hungry until I started. Come on, let's wash up.'

James rose swiftly, shaking his head decisively.

'Not tonight. I'll put the remains of the food in the fridge, and the dishes in the sink, but all you need to do is find something to put on the record player while I get the coffee percolating.'

Eleanor made no protest. Tonight James's wish was her command, and while he put the cups out she looked around for the record player, without success.

'Where *is* the record player, James?'

'You see what looks like a Queen Anne chest near the small window? It actually houses my hi-fi equipment, those drawers are false ones. The records are stacked on the shelf beneath the left-hand window.'

Eleanor rummaged through the pile happily and finally selected some lush music from Henry Mancini.

'Mood music,' said James, putting the coffee tray on the round table. 'Have some brandy with your coffee; no cream, I'm afraid, I'd hardly hoped to have a visitor this evening. Let me put the record on for you.'

'Thank you. Your equipment looks a little bit technical for me.'

They drank their coffee in harmonious silence, and Eleanor sipped her brandy slowly, refusing a second one.

James put her cup and glass back on the tray with his, then he drew her close and they lay relaxed, her head on his shoulder as they listened to the sweet evocative music softly filling the room.

'Eleanor.'

'Yes, James?' She stirred against him lazily.

'How much do you like my bachelor retreat?'

Eleanor looked up at him, searching his face, which seemed paler than usual, making his eyes look dark.

'It's quite perfect. I wouldn't change one thing.'

He pulled her against him and buried his face in her hair.

'Do you like it enough to share it with me? At weekends, at least.'

Eleanor gently freed herself and sat very still for a few moments, staring down at the toes of her grubby plimsolls. When she turned back to him she looked at him squarely.

'Yes.'

He let out a great sigh, and she realised, touched, that he had been holding his breath.

'You're sure, my darling?'

She nodded mutely and lifted her mouth to his.

For some time there was no further sound in the room but the music, then the record ended. There was silence while he kissed her, with tenderness at first, then with growing heat and passion, until they were both pressed close together, mouth to mouth, his hands urgent on the curves of her body until it seemed a natural progression for him to slide it beneath his own almost prone on the settee. Eleanor offered no resistance. The time for defence was gone, her surrender unconditional as her hands and mouth became as urgent as his. She stared up at him with glazed, uncomprehending eyes when at length he tore himself away from her and propped himself above her, balanced with a hand on either side of her waist, his face taut and his eyes almost black with the emotion he was fighting to suppress.

'No?' she whispered.

'No.' James managed a crooked grin. 'How I was able to say that I will never know. Up you come!'

'Did I do something wrong?' Eleanor was assailed with a feeling she dimly realised was frustration. 'James—do you think we'll ever get synchronised on this sex thing and both say yes at the same time?'

He held her close, laughing a little unsteadily.

'That you can be very sure of. For the moment, however, I want to give you something I bought for you in Rio.'

He got up and reached into the pocket of the jacket he'd thrown down on the other settee. Bringing back a small box he opened it, took her left hand in his and, very gently, a question in his eyes, he slid off her wedding ring and replaced it with the ring from the box. Eleanor looked down in disbelief at the oblong baguette ruby flanked either side by three small diamonds. The glittering stones swam hazily through the mist of tears that gathered in her eyes and fell down on to her hand, despite all her efforts to hold them back.

James turned her wet face ruefully up to his.

'I thought I'd managed to dry you out once already this evening, my love. Is the thought of marrying me so doleful a prospect?'

Eleanor's smile glimmered through her tears and she gave an inelegant sniff.

'I had no idea you had marriage in mind.'

'Eleanor, Eleanor,' he said reprovingly, 'do you mean you in fact consented just to shack up with me?'

She nodded, colour flooding her face.

'I really think we ought to do it the conventional way, love.' James's voice was full of laughter. 'And you a vicar's daughter, too, not to mention the reactions of my parents, and Harriet and Richard.' He paused, hesitated, then went on, 'Unless, of course, the experience of the first time has made you wary. I wouldn't attempt to take his place, you know, just try to make you happy in my own way.'

Eleanor pushed her hair back from her damp face and, to James's surprise and delight kissed him hard, her hands either side of his face. She smiled at him saucily.

'I'll be completely honest, darling, there was nothing like that in my mind at all. I presumed you were offering me bed and board, as it were, and I was quite prepared to accept, on any terms you liked. It sounds a bit shameless, put like that, but no way do I ever want to live through another period like the time since we returned from Rio. In certain ways they've been the worst of my life, even worse than when Nick died. I thought I'd lost my miraculous second chance by being so missish in Rio, and you wouldn't want me any more.' She stopped and wiped away more tears childishly with her knuckles. 'I can't tell you how wildly happy I feel to know you want marriage, James, because I want to spend as much of the rest of my life with you as possible.'

The colour ran dark along James's cheekbones and he snatched her against him in a rib-cracking embrace. They lay locked in each other's arms, eyes closed, faces pressed hard together, their bodies unmoving in the inexpressible happiness of mutual love that borders on anguish. After a very, very long time he put her gently away from him and stood up.

'I'm taking you home, my love. Tomorrow we'll tell Mother and Dad and Harriet and Richard, in fact anyone who cares to listen, but tonight is ours, just you and I.' He buttoned up her jacket as if she were a child, kissing each eyelid as he finished. 'Don't make me wait too long, Eleanor. Be merciful and make it soon.'

Eleanor gave the matter serious thought.

'Today is Thursday,' she said slowly. 'I need something to wear, and I suppose we'll have to arrange some sort of reception. Actually, James, I don't think it's possible before Saturday week.'

He stared at her incredulously.

'Do you mean it?'

'Of course not, darling, I was only teasing. Besides, you have to have banns called, although I suppose one can have a special licence.' Eleanor had been smiling, but she became serious as she realised James was in deadly earnest. 'There's no real reason why not, if—if you really want it that soon.'

'I've never wanted anything more in my life.' His voice was quiet, but he spoke with such conviction that

Eleanor took a deep breath and smiled at him radiantly, her heart in her eyes.

'See you in church, then, if you can get a licence.'

'Leave all that to me. I imagine Mother and Harriet can organise the rest.'

Abruptly James picked her up and spun her round crazily.

'Darling girl, I'd better take you home right now—we have a lot to get through before Saturday week.'

'I don't know whether my boss will grant me leave yet.' Eleanor cast a look up at him from beneath her eyelashes. 'Though I'm willing to work overtime, provided the incentive's right!'

# CHAPTER TEN

ELEANOR woke up next morning suddenly and completely, instantly aware that something momentous had happened. She turned on the light to see the time and caught her breath as she saw the blaze of stones on her finger. It was still only five o'clock, and she sank back on the pillows, her hand raised in front of her so that she could gaze at the exquisite ring. She stared at it for a long time, her hand growing cold in the chill atmosphere of pre-dawn while the first golden glow of happiness began to recede and the unwelcome, but only too familiar, irritants of doubt and insecurity wormed their way in to replace it.

She had been very precipitate last night. What on earth had possessed her to lay herself bare like that, to strip her soul naked before someone who was still partly a stranger to her, not to mention surrendering herself physically to such an extent that it was James who had been obliged to call a halt? Her cheeks burned as she tried to shut out the memory of those few brief ecstatic minutes where there had been nothing in the world but James's mouth and his hands and his voice telling her things that were etched in her mind for ever. Anyone less like a paragon would be hard to imagine. She turned over convulsively and buried her face in the pillows.

How can I go through with it? she thought. I've been my own person for so long—one can't count the pathetically brief time I was Nick's wife. On the other hand, if she could ever pluck up the courage to tell

James she had changed her mind—a shudder ran through Eleanor at the mere thought—what then would she have to look forward to? If no man had caught her interest before meeting James there was precious little likelihood of anyone ever doing so in the future. She would just have to resign herself to perpetual so-called single blessedness and the arid life of the eternal maiden aunt.

Eleanor shuddered and closed her eyes against the prospect. James's face was immediate and vivid in her mind, with the look in his blue eyes she had never seen before last night. Slowly, with growing comprehension, she realised what it was—the intent, almost incandescent look of a man very deeply in love. The revelation brought hot tears from beneath her tightly closed lids, to trickle a scalding path down her cheeks.

How could she have even considered that the thought of a life spent solitary in a little flat, secure from the world with her books and records, could be in any possible way preferable to the challenge and splendour of marrying James? She sniffed loudly and sprang out of bed to find a handkerchief, rubbing her eyes fiercely. Why care if she was delivering herself up, body and soul? Despite all the talk of militant feminists and Women's Lib., was that not secretly what the majority of women still hoped to do from the moment they were old enough to realise there were two sexes?

Complete certainty came streaming back in a warm, reassuring wave. Forget about your inhibitions, stupid, she told herself. You have the supreme good fortune to be engaged to an exciting, intelligent, loving man, and very shortly you're going to start spending the rest of your life with him. No more doubts and introspection, just get down on your knees and thank God for a second chance; a good many people don't even get a first.

Singing in a husky, off-key voice, Eleanor showered and dressed in leisurely fashion, even going to the trouble of preparing herself a proper breakfast. With each moment that passed her certainty increased, until by the time she was ready to leave her whole attention was centred on the one important fact in life. In five minutes or so she would see James.

A look from the window in her sitting-room showed the long black car already waiting at the gate, and she threw on her coat, snatching her bag as she tore out of the room and down the stairs, for once forgetting her usual effort to be quiet. She flew down the path and into the passenger seat of the Porsche, turning like a homing-bird into James's waiting arms, and lifted her mouth to be kissed. After a highly satisfactorily interval he held her a little away from him and examined her glowing face intently.

'You look positively luminous.' He kissed the tip of Eleanor's nose and fastened her safety-belt.

'Someone found the switch,' she agreed happily, her eyes still on his face as he drove off. 'You look rather gorgeous yourself.' She laughed as he threw a startled look at her. 'I love you, you love me. Why shouldn't I tell you how attractive you are?'

James put out a hand and captured one of hers.

'I'm not complaining. I'd just prefer to be in sur-roundings that allowed me to do rather more than hold your hand by way of appreciation. Besides, I'm not accustomed to ladies who pay me compliments.'

To Eleanor's delight there was colour in his face, contrasting sharply with the pristine white of his collar.

With an effort he centred all his attention on his driving.

'I'll take you to have lunch with Mother and Dad today. They're expecting me for my usual rundown on things in London, so I thought it would be a good idea to produce you as a surprise so that we can break the news together.'

Eleanor looked up from fascinated contemplation of her ring.

'Will that be all right, to land your mother with an unexpected guest?' she asked doubtfully.

'My mother may have faults—none worth mentioning, I may add—but her catering capabilities don't number among them, I assure you.' He grinned, looking suddenly boyish. 'Besides, I shall take great pleasure in springing our surprise, although I have a feeling Dad won't be too astonished, somehow.'

Eleanor removed her ring regretfully and replaced it in its box, which she carefully put away in a zipped pocket of her handbag.

'Hey!' James noticed what she was doing. 'Aren't you going to keep that on?'

'It's agony to hide it away,' Eleanor assured him, 'but I'd rather wait until we tell your mother and father. While we're on that subject, James, will you take me over to Harriet's this evening? I'd like us to break the glad news to them both in person too.'

'Ring her up as soon as we get in and arrange something,' said James promptly. 'For my part I want my badge of ownership on your finger as soon as possible. Or does that offend your feminist principles?'

'Not in the least.' Eleanor was honest. 'I do belong to you, and I—I like it. Why should I pretend otherwise?'

James released his possessive grip on her hand just before they entered the office building, and they proceded through the hall very sedately, running the gamut of morning greetings with circumspection, blissfully unaware of the smiling looks of comprehension directed after them.

As soon as Eleanor had dealt with the morning post she rang Harriet's number.

'Where on earth did you get to last night?' Her sister's voice was indignant. 'Mrs Jenkins had some story about your dashing back to the office. I can't think why you don't keep a bed there and be done with it. Are you feeling better?'

'I forgot to lock something up, that's all,' said Eleanor soothingly, 'and, for the last part, I think I can report a hundred percent improvement.'

'I can tell that by your voice.' Harriet was patently much relieved. 'Are you coming tomorrow for the weekend?'

Eleanor paused for a moment, then asked.

'Is it convenient for me to come tonight? May I bring James for a meal?'

The silence at the other end of the line was so prolonged Eleanor began to think it had gone dead.

'Of course, El,' said Harriet eventually, 'but I did rather feel things weren't exactly rosy after you came back from Rio. With tremendous effort I nobly refrained from enquiring whether you'd quarrelled, because you looked so off colour.'

'I did notice,' said Eleanor drily. 'And of course you were dead right. We'd had rather a spectacular row, in fact, but now we've—well we've made it up. See you about eight, then; nothing too special, Harriet, don't go slaving over a hot stove and all that.'

'Don't talk rubbish, love. See you tonight.'

The smile on Eleanor's face took on added warmth as she put the phone down and saw James standing in the doorway, watching her. He was attractively formal in dark blue suit and navy and white spotted foulard tie against his white shirt.

'I keep pinching myself to see if I'm awake, James.'
He crossed the room and kissed her briefly.

'If you need convincing, angel, this way is preferable, but I assure you it's strictly for real. Now, I hate to bring you down to earth, but can I have that report, please?'

The rest of the day passed swiftly, partly due to their extremely protracted lunch hour with the senior Ramsays. The latter were so very delighted at the news that Eleanor was close to tears, especially when, with the air of a genial conjuror, Hector produced a bottle of champagne to celebrate the occasion in style.

'I had a feeling we might be needing it,' he told them, with the irrepresible twinkle in his eyes. 'Knew you were right for each other from the first moment I saw you together.'

The ring now officially on her finger, Eleanor really felt she and James were well and truly engaged, particularly as he insisted on announcing it personally to the entire staff of Ramsay & Coulter. The afternoon was mainly given up to receiving delighted congratulations. Frances was so pleased that her eyes were frankly wet as she embraced Eleanor and congratulated James.

'How much time are you giving me to collect for a wedding present from the staff?' she asked, smiling widely.

'About a week, if possible, certainly not more than two, at the most.' James grinned at her startled expression, then looked at Eleanor, his expression clear for all to read. 'I see no possible reason why I should wait longer than that.'

Eleanor felt the colour rise in her face, but the look she returned steadily made James move to take her hand, and made Frances swallow a lump in her throat.

'O.K.,' she said flippantly. 'What do you fancy— toast rack, pickle jar or a garden gnome?'

'Just the thing,' said James absently, his mind so obviously taken up with other things that Frances went silently from the room, smiling to herself, the other two oblivious to her departure.

When James brought the Porsche to a halt in the Lords' drive just after eight that evening, Eleanor was rapidly becoming accustomed to the change in tempo of her hitherto quiet, well-ordered life-style.

'You know, James, I can't help feeling a bit like Cinderella. This time last night I was in rags, so to speak, and tonight, here I am in my party gear, with this fabulous ring on my finger, and last but not least, with Prince Charming as my escort.'

James grimaced at the last bit and put his hands either side of her face, looking down at her with eyes full of tenderness.

'Only the car won't turn into a pumpkin, princess, and I promise you there won't be a nasty transformation scene at midnight. Now kiss me properly before we go in.'

Eleanor obeyed with fervour, and it was with some reluctance that James drew away and turned to haul her weekend case from the back of the car as the front door of the house flew open silhouetting the trim figure of Harriet against the oblong of light.

She drew them into the warm hall and plied them with drinks, Harriet's bright eyes darting speculative glances from James to Eleanor while she excused Richard's non-appearance owing to his late arrival home from evening surgery.

'He's changing,' she said, waving them to a settee in the living room. She looked pointedly from Eleanor's red silk dress and iridescent jacket to her own black velvet slacks and black and white printed chiffon shirt. 'Am I grand enough—shall I change?' Her eyes were brimming with mischief as she called to Richard as he came into the room.

'Thank heavens you're reasonably smart, darling. I had sudden visions of you in your old golf sweater or something, and just look at Eleanor, not to mention James in that superb velvet jacket.'

Richard was unperturbed.

'I don't think our guests will really mind what we're wearing, as long as the drinks and the food are good. Talking of which, let me give you refills.' He shook hands with James, kissed Eleanor and provided them with the necessary drinks.

'Eleanor tells me this is the only red dress she owns,' said James, with a smile at her that made Harriet blink, 'and apparently this evening it was femininely imperative that she wear red to match this.'

With a wide grin of pure triumph he lifted Eleanor's hand, which she had managed to keep hidden, and proudly showed the other two the beautiful ruby she wore in place of her wedding ring.

Harriet's screech of delight was audible a mile away, according to Richard later, as she threw herself at them both in a frenzy of hugs and kisses. Richard's less demonstrative congratulations were equally sincere, albeit tempered with regret that there was no champagne in the house. James, however, had come prepared, and went out to the car to bring in the four bottles that were his contribution to the evening. Harriet then had the brainwave of ringing up Hector and Margaret Ramsay, insisting that they come to join in celebrating the festive occasion, and James set off to fetch them immediately. It was a highly convivial group that eventually sat down to dinner that evening, James in frank possession of Eleanor's hand at all possible moments, and Eleanor's face lit with such radiance that

Harriet was obliged to retire to the kitchen at intervals to blow her nose and take a surreptitious swipe at her eyes on the pretext of seeing to the meal.

At the end of the evening it was unanimously decided to call a taxi for James and his parents, leaving the Porsche to be collected next day, in view of the quantity and variety of the evening's alcoholic intake. James and Eleanor were tactfully left alone to say goodnight, and he kissed her lingeringly, holding her close.

'Not too many more goodnights, angel,' he whispered against her hair. 'Just a week or so and then I'll have sole rights in taking care of the happy-ever-after clause in our marriage contract.'

'Oh, James,' she sighed, 'I wish it were tomorrow!'

'Not as much as I do, darling. Sleep well and dream of me.'

When the door had closed behind James and his parents, Eleanor looked at Harriet, who held out her arms and hugged her tightly, for once not saying a word. Richard gently put an arm about them both and slowly shepherded them to bed, brushing aside half-hearted protests about clearing up.

'Tomorrow,' he pronounced firmly. 'I for one don't intend to spoil my rosy glow by washing up!'

# CHAPTER ELEVEN

ON the morning of her wedding Eleanor opened her eyes slowly and stretched, yawning. She sat up abruptly at the sigh of Harriet approaching with a heavily-laden tray.

''Morning, love.' Harriet beamed at her happily. 'It's a bit cold, but the sun is breaking through, and frankly I thought you'd have been awake hours ago. It's nine o'clock, sleepyhead; come on, you're getting married at twelve!'

Eleanor grinned back and stretched again luxuriously as Harriet plumped up pillows behind her and took the tray from the bedside table to place it across Eleanor's knees.

'It was hardly likely to have slipped my mind! I woke about five, actually, and I've been dozing on and off since then, but I must have fallen asleep about eight o'clock quite soundly; not very bride-like, I suppose.' She inspected the contents of the tray with awe. 'Am I supposed to eat all this? I *would* rather like to fit into my wedding dress!'

'Pooh, of course you can, can't have you fainting in church,' said Harriet airily. 'Besides, I rather fancy you're going to have to share some of it. My lot were too excited to eat any breakfast this morning. I had my work cut out keeping them from invading your room at the crack of dawn. Here, let me have the cereal dish. Now finish the bacon and egg. I made mountains of toast, because I thought I'd share some. I brought two cups, so I can filch some tea as well.'

Harriet settled herself comfortably on the end of the bed, munching her toast and surveying Eleanor with an assessing look.

'Well, how's the bride? No traditional jitters?'

Eleanor was quiet for a moment.

'Not any more.' She looked up at Harriet candidly. 'I must confess there was the odd tremor of doubt, even after I said the fatal yes.'

'Doubts about your feelings for James?' Harriet's eyes were troubled.

'No.' Eleanor shook her head positively. 'Never that. Believe it or not, despite all that guerilla warfare that went on initially, it was really a case of one look and wham, however much I tried to deceive myself. It was the same for James too, he tells me—quite repeatedly, in fact.'

She coloured a little and poured herself more tea.

Harriet let out the breath she had been unconsciously holding.

'Thank heavens! You had me worried there for a moment.' She paused. 'What was it, then, love?'

'Well, I'm not a teenager, Harriet, I'm supposed to be reasonably mature.' Eleanor smiled ruefully. 'But I haven't exactly had a great deal of experience of the opposite sex, have I?'

'I should think James is highly satisfied with that arrangement, surely!'

'I don't mean in the physical sense. I'm not putting things very clearly. What I'm trying to explain, Harriet, is that I love him so much it makes me apprehensive, gives me the feeling of being minus the outer skin I've cultivated over my emotions. It's a bit awesome to feel dependent for one's whole future happiness on just one person.'

Harriet was silent for a little before answering, then

she looked at Eleanor squarely.

'That depends entirely on the person. I did just that and I've never had reason to regret it for a moment. That's what marriage is all about, I suppose, total commitment, but something of a gamble too. Perhaps poor Nick would have been the ideal partner, I don't know. As you well know, I always had reservations. I was never convinced that you had more than a brother-and-sister relationship going for you, and apart from that you were both so young. Now James is something else, isn't he?'

Eleanor nodded, an unguarded expression of sensual appreciation in her eye as James's face and voice were pictured in her inner eye for a fleeting second; though not so fleeting that it was missed by Harriet, with private amusement.

'One last thing, El. Marriage is a two-way relationship. Don't forget you hold just the same control over James's happiness, too. If ever a man was head over heels in love, he is. You haven't seen the look on his face when he thinks you're unaware. Today in church you're both going to promise to love and cherish each other, and I'm perfectly sure neither of you will have any problem in keeping that promise.' Harriet grinned. 'Here endeth the first and last lesson!'

Eleanor smiled back with gratitude.

'They were just very minor qualms, really. James is everything I could wish for in a husband—I'm a very fortunate lady.'

'He's a very dishy man, darling, but at the risk of sounding sickeningly smug, I'm afraid he doesn't hold a candle to Richard!'

Eleanor hurled a pillow at her sister in protest, but Harriet dodged and caught it neatly with the ease of long practice.

'You'll have that tray over, you nitwit!' she shrieked.

'Never mind the tray,' said Eleanor, then deliberately raised the atmosphere to a more frivolous level. 'How has my hairdo survived?' She craned to see herself in the dressing-table mirror.

'It looks fabulous. That girl in town coped very well with the Rio haircut—she didn't do a bad job on mine either.' Harriet craned her neck to preen a little in the mirror.

'Just pray our hats will stay on top. Ah, don't look now, Harriet, but I think your dire prophesy is about to be fulfilled, the door is opening crack by crack.'

'Come in, you lot.' Their mother was resigned. 'Ask Auntie El if she can spare some toast, and please try to confine it to your mouths rather than the duvet. Where's Victoria?'

'She's in her high chair, talking to Mrs Jenkins,' said Edward, shepherding the other two tray-wards. 'You really don't mind if we have some, Auntie El?'

'I really don't,' his aunt assured him lovingly. 'Feel free—have it all, I've finished.'

'Victoria can't talk really,' Charles felt bound to point out, after giving it some thought.

'I know that,' said his elder brother, exasperated, 'but she and Mrs Jenkins sort of—sort of com—com . . .'

'Communicate?' suggested Eleanor tactfully. 'By the way, Harriet, it was a stroke of genius having Mrs Jenkins over to stay last night. She was over the moon when I asked her.'

'She's been invaluable. Between them she and my Mrs Morris have made the house look superb already—that's why I hope you don't mind this lot up here with you. They just might keep out of mischief that way.'

'Mrs Jenkins likes me,' said David positively, climbing on the bed to cuddle up to Eleanor, his eyes fixed firmly on the last piece of toast, 'she gives me things to eat.'

'One biscuit and you're anyone's,' said his mother. 'Mind Auntie El's hairdo!'

'Not to worry, it will stand up to a lot more cuddling than that.' Eleanor hugged the little boy.

'Which,' said Harriet, picking up the tray, a wicked look in her eye, 'all things considered, is just as well!'

'That will do, Harriet. *Pas devant les enfants.*'

'Nonsense! May as well get used to the facts of life first as last. Now, fascinating as all this is, I really think I'd better put out the food. At least the cold weather makes that part of it easier. Mrs Ramsay has sent round the most mouth-watering vol-au-vents; lobster, El, and she's made a superb angel-cake, not to mention the jumbo-sized cold turkey that arrived last night. She's really enjoying herself. I gather Hector is as smug as if he'd engineered the whole thing himself.'

'He's quite sure he did!' said Eleanor dryly. 'Harriet, I can't help wishing you'd let me have my way and had the reception at a hotel or something. I'm so afraid all this catering is going to exhaust you, even with the extra help.'

Harriet stood still in the doorway, her vivid face for once serious.

'You can't imagine how much I'm revelling in it, El. After the last time, which was such a hurried little affair—no reception, no guests. Anyone would have thought we were ashamed of the whole thing. This time it will be different—as perfect as we can possibly make it. Now get a move on and have your bath, do you realise it's nearly ten already? Come on, you lot, I'd better start getting you into shape too.'

Eleanor lay quiet for a little while longer after Harriet had rounded up her sons and led them inexorably off to be scrubbed. It was inevitable that her mind turned to thoughts of that other far-off wedding with Nick. It had been a hurried little affair, ignored by his parents. Only Harriet and Richard, and Nick's college room-mate as best man, had been in the familiar old church, where the unfamiliar new curate had married them somewhat hastily so that they could dash off in Nick's old car to catch the ferry from Dover en route for Spain. All their pooled funds had been splurged on the two-week honeymoon, so Eleanor had merely worn her newest summer frock with a hat borrowed from Harriet, who had been unable to hide the tears as the young pair drove away. The sadness of the memory was tempered by the certainty that Nick would want her to be happy, and Eleanor began on the preparations for her wedding day with the tranquil conviction that today nothing would happen to cast a shadow on her joy.

Despite Harriet's gloomy prognostications that no one would be ready on time, it was exactly eleven-thirty when Eleanor took a final look in the mirror in Harriet's room and decided she was ready. She would secretly have loved to wear long white satin and a lace veil. Instead her dress was short, arrow-slim, with high neck and long sleeves in fine white wool, worn beneath a hip-length loose collarless jacket with sleeves ending in great cuffs of snow-lynx fur. Eleanor had resisted all Harriet's entreaties to wear a fur hat to match, and on top of the gleaming, dark feathery hair she had a small severe white felt pillbox, its sole concession to bridal frivolity a white frosting of veil that just skimmed her eyebrows. She picked up gloves in coffee-coloured suede to match her delicate shoes, and finally pinned on James's flowers, two creamy, beige-spotted orchids.

Eleanor started down the stairs to find the rest of the family imbibing various beverages in the hall. Three smart little boys in blazers were very much amused at their father's grey top hat, while Victoria, resplendent in white furry hooded coat, sat placidly on Mrs Jenkins's arm. The latter was clad in her churchgoing best coat, plus an amazing violet-trimmed toque reminiscent of the late Queen Mary. Harriet came hurrying in from the dining-room, superbly elegant in a tawny velvet coat topped by a dashing red fox hat. She stopped short as she saw Eleanor hesitating at the top of the stairs, and everyone looked up. There was a little silence, then Richard came forward to meet her, hand outstretched.

'Your chariot awaits, Snow Queen, but there's just time for a fortifying sherry before we set off.'

'Oh, Eleanor,' breathed Harriet, kissing her cheek with infinite care, 'you look utterly ravishing—and I will *not* cry, or I'll spoil my make-up and drip on my velvet. Mrs Jenkins, don't you dare cry either!'

'No, of course not,' said that lady, sniffing valiantly. 'But it's a bit difficult, there's something about a bride. No, my pet,' to a struggling Victoria, 'you can't go to Auntie Eleanor just now, you come in the big car with Mummy and me, and the boys too.'

Harriet swept them all off, leaving Eleanor and Richard to finish their sherry in peace.

'Here's to you, little sister.' Richard touched his glass to hers. 'This time may everything be roses.'

Eleanor lifted an eyebrow.

'A few thorns as well, I imagine, Richard, and

doubtless there'll be the odd fight or two.'

'Naturally, if only for the considerable pleasure of making up. Nevertheless, even to my unimaginative eye the pair of you obviously belong together, which is the best prescription for a happy marriage. So let's be off, love, and get you started on the first step.'

By just after six that evening Eleanor and James were in the Porsche making their way into the Cotswolds at a leisurely pace. They had been waved off by a very gay company of wedding guests who were obviously all set to go on celebrating for the rest of the evening. As soon as the outskirts of the town were left behind James turned into a layby and stopped the car.

'Forgotten something, darling?' Eleanor smiled at him lovingly in the dim light from the dashboard.

'Not a thing, as far as I know.' James reached for her and took her in his arms, his mouth warm on hers, then he rubbed his nose gently against hers. 'For the past hour, despite the incredible party the reception developed into, I've had the devil's own job in dragging my mind away from thoughts of doing this—and this—and this.' He punctuated his words with small, hard kisses. 'Any objections, Mrs Ramsay?'

She looked up at him, bemused.

'Oh, James, do you realise what you just said?'

'If you mean the regrettable fact that my mind is hardly ever free of the thought of making love to you . . .'

'No, idiot,' she said impatiently, then thought for a moment. 'On second thoughts I don't find that regrettable in the least, actually, but it was being referred to as Mrs Ramsay that really brought it home to me. It sounds so perfect, James.'

'I'm in complete agreement!' His profile looked so

smugly complacent as he started the car that Eleanor had to laugh.

'You look just like the cat that swallowed the cream!'

'I feel that way too, though you might have found a more romantic description. What surprises me is how enjoyable the wedding was. I've always been led to believe it was an experience to dread.'

'Harriet was determined it was going to be the happiest occasion possible, and I think she succeeded admirably—everyone seemed to have a marvellous time. Richard is always the most superb host, of course, but your father was a tower of strength, and your cousin was a highly accomplished best man. He seemed rather dazzled with Harriet, I thought.'

James laughed.

'So was John Coulter, and most of the other men present; she knocks them all for six. Although, today, even Harriet was cast in the shade, as the bride outshone everyone. When you came down the aisle I felt the proudest man on earth.'

They were making for a village in the heart of the Cotswolds, not far from Broadway and Chipping Campden. Originally James had wanted to travel to some exotic location for the honeymoon, but Eleanor had quietly but firmly declined. She was insistent on somewhere near, with the minimum of travelling. James had therefore suggested the maximum of isolation to go with it, thus they were heading for a small holiday cottage owned by friends of the senior Ramsays on the edge of the little village of Cleeve Prior. They reached it shortly before seven, James coaxing the Porsche slowly over the uneven cart track that led to it. The cottage had once been the home of one of the farm labourers working on the large neighbouring farm, and had been preserved with great care practically in its original form, with the added amenities of a bathroom and central heating. It was very small, with one large living room and kitchen downstairs, and a bedroom and bathroom upstairs.

James hefted the suitcases up the steep stairway, narrowly missing contact with the low beam overhead, while Eleanor explored the ground floor. She followed him upstairs after a swift look round, laughing at the muffled curse coming from above.

'I have my brass and chintz here in abundance, darling,' she said as she joined him in the bedroom. 'I love it, though, and I expect there's a heavenly view in the daytime. I must admit I enjoy the warmth, though, the heating is very definitely contemporary!'

Eleanor smiled happily, walking into his outstretched arms and lifting her face to his.

'You were supposed to carry me over the threshold.'

James promptly picked her up and carried her to the bed, grinning at her heightened colour as he set her down on it.

'I'm the sort who likes to get my priorities right,' he informed her, lying close to her and nibbling her lips, her ear, then moving on down her neck. He paused for a moment, leaning on his elbow to look down at her. 'You know, Eleanor, I find it quite odd that you're not kicking and fighting tooth and nail. Does this mean that you've finally surrendered unconditionally?'

Eleanor lay still for a moment, looking into the gleaming blue eyes above her, then wriggled off the bed.

'I did that the night you asked me to marry you, James Ramsay,' she said, looking over her shoulder as she went to the dressing table, 'and it's you who've been the soul of circumspection ever since. Not that we've had much opportunity to be alone together for the past two weeks.'

He followed her and put his arms round her from behind, looking at her in the mirror, his chin on her shoulder.

'My resistance had reached its lowest ebb that night, my beautiful. I've taken great care not to put it to the test again—at least until this precise moment in time.'

His eyes had been holding hers in the mirror, but now their expression made Eleanor drop hers suddenly, heat stealing over her body, coupled with a feeling of intense shyness.

Abruptly James released her and tapped her bottom lightly.

'Come on,' he said briskly, 'it's a lovely night, let's go for a stroll down to the Wheatsheaf in the village. I'll stand you a glass of champagne, if you like.'

Eleanor smiled gratefully.

'You are a lovely man, James, that's just exactly what I'd love to do. We can work up an appetite—for dinner, I mean, stop leering. Shall I need a coat?'

They were both dressed in jeans and sweaters, and as the night was unseasonally mild they set off for the village just as they were, leaving their unpacking for later. They wandered hand-in-hand through the tiny village, which was little more than a handful of cottages, with a post office and general store, an ancient small church and the Wheatsheaf Inn, one of the legion where Shakespeare was supposed to have caroused.

They sat in the little lounge bar near a roaring fire, the pub fairly quiet this early in the evening. Eleanor refused the promised champagne, and settled for a more ordinary white wine. James moved close to her on the high-backed settle, his arm lightly across the back of her shoulders, his mouth occasionally touching her hair. Eleanor began to relax completely, all the tension and excitement of the day receding, leaving in its wake a sense of wellbeing and warm contentment. When James brought her a third drink and settled himself with his arm unashamedly round her waist, she leaned dreamily against him.

'Do you think the landlord knows we're on our honeymoon, James?'

'Would you mind if he did?'

'Not in the slightest. I'd rather like to run through the village shouting "we're married, we're married!" Do you think people would care?'

James finished his whisky quickly and took her glass away.

'How much champagne did you have this afternoon, my sweet? I noticed you hardly ate anything.'

'For one thing those great fur cuffs rather restricted me, and for another I was too excited, but I felt thirsty all the time. Do I look tipsy?' She gazed up at him anxiously.

He smiled down at her slowly with an expression in his eyes that made her bones dissolve.

'Not yet; but I intend to make sure that my bride doesn't pass out on me, so let's have a nice brisk walk back to the cottage.'

Eleanor giggled.

'We'll have to have a big supper. Harriet came down with your mother yesterday with enough food for a month. Perhaps they're expecting us to be snowed in.'

James stood up, giving her his hand, and led her out, calling goodnight to the landlord.

'It's possible they had the idea we might not want to trouble ourselves with the more mundane things in life for a while. Oh, lord, talking of that brisk walk, Eleanor, we're going to have to make a dash for it.'

Even as he was speaking the heavens opened, and they fled through the village in an effort to escape the worst of the deluge of rain. They arrived at the cottage breathless and laughing, looking as though they'd been in the river. In the light of the living room they inspected each other, trying to get their breath back. James's black sweater and jeans were sodden, but Eleanor's jeans were elegant affairs of gold velveteen and had suffered sadly, as had her matching mohair sweater.

'Oh, James,' she wailed, 'my beautiful hairdo!'

He pushed her towards the stairs and directed her up them before him.

'Never mind your hair, you ninny,' he said lovingly, 'get those wet things off and take a hot shower. I haven't preserved you from advanced intoxication only to have you prostrate with pneumonia.'

Eleanor obeyed instantly, and as quickly as possible her wet clothes were stripped off and spread to dry in the airing cupboard in the bathroom. She stood for several minutes in the hot spray of the shower, her head wrapped in a towel, then she rubbed herself fiercely until she glowed. Her hair was a damp cloud round her shoulders, but as there was nothing she could do about that she looked round for something to wrap herself in as she had brought nothing to change into in her headlong flight to the bathroom. She wound a dry red bathtowel round her sarong-fashion, tucking it in beneath her armpits, and went back into the bedroom where James, clad only in wet jeans, was rubbing at his hair with the kitchen towel. He looked at Eleanor and became still. She smiled shyly.

'I didn't take in anything to put on.'

James remained motionless and silent, merely looking at her with the same intense blue gaze. Eleanor knew she was babbling, but felt constrained to keep chattering, if only to break the silence.

'Harriet bought me the most beautiful Janet Reger nightgown and peignoir—I mean, you couldn't possibly term it a dressing gown, honey-coloured wild silk—I should have taken it in with me . . .'

Her voice trailed away as, with the utmost care, he put down the towel he was holding and came slowly towards her. When he spoke his voice was husky, even deeper than usual.

'I'm positive it's everything you say, but from a mere male point of view I can envisage nothing more alluring than what you're wearing right now.' His eyes followed a leisurely path from the bare toes that were curling nervously into the carpet to the mass of tumbled hair. 'I think that what attracts me most is its air of insecurity.'

Then he moved swiftly, his arms tightened round her like steel bands and she was almost deafened by the sound of her heartbeat combined with his as his words were proved accurate and the towel slithered to her feet. A sudden shock of heat rushed over her as she was crushed against his chest and her mouth opened convulsively to the demand of his. Vaguely she was aware of metal clinking as his belt dropped to the floor, then he lifted her and carried her to the bed, laying her down on it with the exquisite care one would accord Meissen china. With no trace of shyness Eleanor held up her arms to James, and he followed her down until their bodies were welded together as every curve of hers melted into every muscle and angle of his.

This time there was no drawing back, as Eleanor was granted entry into a sensuous world where there were only James's hands and mouth, her mind losing ground gladly to her senses until a small corner of her consciousness prodded her. With a superhuman effort she drew her mouth back from his.

'James,' she gasped, 'I want to say something . . .'

He took her face between his hands and looked down into her eyes with a look of such intense love and desire that she was silenced.

'My darling,' his voice was rough, unsteady, 'I will listen to you and talk to you for the rest of our lives, but, at this moment, I just want to love you. Not solely to make love, but to worship you as I promised in church today, body, soul, heart and mind. Everything that is me wants to become one with everything that is you; only right now to become one flesh is overriding everything else. More than anything else in the world I want to hear you feel the same way, Eleanor.'

Eleanor was lost. She feverishly returned his kisses, murmuring between them only what he wanted to hear. Her mind was in complete abeyance, except for one tiny corner which registered with amazement the trembling, moaning, helpless creature who twisted and writhed beneath his mouth and his expert, knowing hands that stroked and smoothed and thrust until she was drugged with desire. So far lost was she that when their bodies finally merged she was utterly unable to control the sharp little cry wrung from her at the first brief burning anguish of his possession.

James's body froze. The muscles of his back were taut as whipcord beneath her fluttering restless hands, and Eleanor's eyes flew open to meet his gazing down into hers with an expression of mixed incredulity and elation.

'Eleanor!' His voice was hoarse, unbelieving.

She dug her fingernails into his back and spoke through clenched teeth.

'You just said that now was the time for love, James. So don't talk. Love me. Don't stop.'

'I couldn't if I tried,' he gasped, and with infinite care his body began to initiate hers slowly into the mystery that had hitherto been only speculation. She was a willing pupil, quickly learning the lesson so expertly taught, caught up in the rhythmic force of pure sensation that was almost impossible to bear. And yet there was something that still eluded her.

'Please, James, please!' she sobbed until his mouth came down hard on hers and what she begged for was granted as the involuntary heat of fulfilment flooded them both and slowly receded, leaving them clasped tightly in each other's arms like survivors of a shipwreck thrown up on the shore.

Their heartbeats and their breathing gradually slowed down. James covered them both with the duvet, turning on his side to draw her close against him, her head on his shoulder.

'You tried to tell me and I wouldn't listen.' He was remorseful. 'The last thing I expected was that you were inexperienced. Did I hurt you, sweetheart?'

Eleanor raised her head and smiled at him slumbrously.

'Hardly at all. In fact a negligible price to pay for what followed. Thank you for making it so beautiful for me, James.'

He stroked the wildly disordered hair back from her forehead.

'Do you feel like telling me now what I so rudely refused to listen to before, Eleanor?'

She settled herself even more closely against him, and began a little hesitantly.

'Nick and I were married very rapidly, with no reception, because Nick wanted to get off for Dover to catch the ferry for the Continent. His car was rather old and the tyres had a blow-out on the motorway and we crashed into the central reservation. Just previously I'd climbed into the back of the car to open a picnic hamper, which undoubtedly saved my life. I escaped with severe concussion, multiple bruising and a broken wrist. Nick was killed instantly. It was just two hours after the wedding.'

The arms holding her close tightened protectively.

'What I find hard to understand is that you say there's been no one else since. You were only eighteen, surely there've been men who would have jumped at the chance of taking you out?'

'In college they all thought I was married. It was easier to let it go like that. Since then Harriet and Richard have pushed every eligible male they could find in my direction, but I've never been in the least interested. Then I looked up from your father's shoulder and saw you eyeing me with such distaste and that was that.'

'And I should think so too!' James's voice was teasing, then became serious. 'Do you know, angel, at this moment I wouldn't change places with any other man on earth. You gave me a very unexpected wedding present, Eleanor Ramsay.'

'You must admit that it was rather a difficult snippet of information to bring up in the course of ordinary conversation!' Eleanor chuckled into his smooth bare chest. 'Put yourself in my place—oh, well, of course you couldn't, could you in this case, but how was I to say on my wedding night, "By the way, darling, I thought you'd like to know I'm the only twenty-four-year-old virgin left in captivity"?'

'Be as flip as you like—it's made me feel about ten feet tall. Where do you think you're going?' as

Eleanor made to move away.

'I'm going to array myself in my aforementioned honeymoon rig and do something about feeding you.'

She was yanked back into his arms.

'Later. In fact, much later. I can eat any time.' James held her captive while his mouth roamed over her face and neck, and his hands began to pursue their slow, tantalising path from shoulder to breasts, to hips and to innumerable places all over that Eleanor had never dreamed would be so vulnerable and responsive.

'James.' She spoke with difficulty, her body involuntarily thrusting itself against his. His hands and mouth paused in their quest for a moment.

'What is it, my darling?'

'There's a lot to be said for British workmanship after all.'

James propped himself up on one elbow in astonishment.

'Very patriotic, I'm sure, but why the devil did you bring that up at a moment like this? A bride is supposed to be melting and warm. Responsive. Co-operative.' He punctuated each word with kisses that sent the now familiar tremors racing through her.

'Well, to put it another way, my love—oh, James, please wait a moment, I can't think when you do that. I merely wanted to point out that it's a good thing we didn't return to Rio for our honeymoon. In the light of my recent experience I don't really feel the beds would ever have stood up to it.'

Convulsed with laughter, they clung to each other until the hilarity died away and they began to lose themselves in each other to the extent that it was quite immaterial whether they were in Rio, the Cotswolds or on the moon.

 **ROMANCE**

# Next month's romances from Mills & Boon

Each month, you can choose from a world of variety in romance with Mills & Boon. These are the new titles to look out for next month.

**WEDDING OF THE YEAR** Anne Weale
**A PASSIONATE AFFAIR** Anne Mather
**COUNTERFEIT BRIDE** Sara Craven
**THIS TIME IS FOR EVER** Sheila Strutt
**PASSIONATE INTRUDER** Lilian Peake
**A DREAM CAME TRUE** Betty Neels
**THE MAN SHE MARRIED** Violet Winspear
**BOUGHT WITH HIS NAME** Penny Jordan
**MAN FROM THE KIMBERLEYS** Margaret Pargeter
**HANDMAID TO MIDAS** Jane Arbor
**DEVIL IN DISGUISE** Jessica Steele
**MELT A FROZEN HEART** Lindsay Armstrong

Buy them from your usual paperback stockist, or write to: Mills & Boon Reader Service, P.O. Box 236, Thornton Rd, Croydon, Surrey CR9 3RU, England. Readers in South Africa-write to: Mills & Boon Reader Service of Southern Africa, Private Bag X3010, Randburg, 2125.

## Mills & Boon
### the rose of romance

# ROMANCE

# Variety is the spice of romance

Each month, Mills & Boon publish new romances. New stories about people falling in love. A world of variety in romance – from the best writers in the romantic world. Choose from these titles in November.

**NORTHERN SUNSET** Penny Jordan
**A LAMP FOR JONATHAN** Essie Summers
**SPELLBOUND** Margaret Way
**LUCIFER'S BRAND** Nicola West
**THE DEVIL'S MISTRESS** Sarah Holland
**PASSION FROM THE PAST** Carole Mortimer
**A TRADITION OF PRIDE** Janet Dailey
**A MAN OF MEANS** Kay Thorpe
**MAN FOR HIRE** Sally Wentworth
**SPRING FEVER** Kerry Allyne
**ARCTIC ENEMY** Linda Harrel
**RELUCTANT PARAGON** Catherine George

On sale where you buy paperbacks. If you require further information or have any difficulty obtaining them, write to: Mills & Boon Reader Service, PO Box 236, Thornton Road, Croydon, Surrey CR9 3RU, England.

# Mills & Boon
## the rose of romance

# FREE-an exclusive Anne Mather title, MELTING FIRE

At Mills & Boon we value very highly the opinion of our readers. What you tell us about what you like in romantic reading is important to us.

So if you will tell us which Mills & Boon romance you have most enjoyed reading lately, we will send you a copy of MELTING FIRE by Anne Mather – absolutely FREE.

There are no snags, no hidden charges. It's absolutely FREE.

Just send us your answer to our question, and help us to bring you the best in romantic reading.

CLAIM YOUR FREE BOOK NOW

Simply fill in details below, cut out and post to: Mills & Boon Reader Service, FREEPOST, P.O. Box 236, Croydon, Surrey CR9 9EL

The Mills & Boon story I have most enjoyed during the past 6 months is

TITLE _____

AUTHOR_____ BLOCK LETTERS, PLEASE

NAME (Mrs/Miss) _____ EP4

ADDRESS _____

_____ POST CODE _____

Offer restricted to ONE Free Book a year per household. Applies only in U.K. and Eire.
CUT OUT AND POST TODAY – NO STAMP NEEDED

## Mills & Boon
### the rose of romance